DETROIT PUBLIC LIBRARY
3 5674 03690736 9

“Decision time.” He pulled her closer to him, but this time he took her mouth in a kiss that nipped at her lower lip before deepening into an erotic assault on her senses.

Warmth spread through her as his mouth left hers and trailed over her cheek, then her throat, before returning to her lips in a swift final kiss. He stepped back a pace, letting go of her, and she felt the loss in every fiber of her being.

“So?” he said levelly, fa [illegible] onless.
“What's it [illegible]

“You sai [illegible] sted
weakly. [illegible]

“I said I [illegible] nto bed
with me, [illegible] gently. “I didn't
say anything about kissing or cuddling or a whole host of other…pleasant things between friends.”

D0834460

Library on Wheels
3666 Grand River Avenue
Detroit, Michigan 48208

NOV - 2012

HELEN BROOKS was born and educated in Northampton, England. She met her husband at the age of sixteen and thirty-five years later the magic is still there. They have three lovely children and three beautiful grandchildren.

Helen began writing in 1990 as she approached that milestone of a birthday—forty! She realized that her two teenage ambitions (writing a novel and learning to drive) had been lost amid babies and family life, so she set about resurrecting them. Her first novel was accepted after one rewrite, and she passed her driving test (the former was a joy and the latter an unmitigated nightmare).

Helen is a committed Christian and fervent animal lover. She finds time is always at a premium, but somehow she fits in walks in the countryside with her husband and their Irish terrier, meals out followed by the cinema or theater, reading, swimming and visiting with friends. She also enjoys sitting in her wonderfully therapeutic, rambling old garden in the sun with a glass of red wine (under the guise of resting while thinking, of course!).

Since becoming a full-time writer Helen has found her occupation one of pure joy. She loves exploring what makes people tick and finds the old adage "truth is stranger than fiction" to be absolutely true. She would love to hear from any readers, care of Harlequin Presents®.

SWEET SURRENDER WITH THE MILLIONAIRE

HELEN BROOKS

~ BRITISH BACHELORS ~

Library on Wheels
3666 Grand River Avenue
Detroit, Michigan 48208

TORONTO • NEW YORK • LONDON
AMSTERDAM • PARIS • SYDNEY • HAMBURG
STOCKHOLM • ATHENS • TOKYO • MILAN • MADRID
PRAGUE • WARSAW • BUDAPEST • AUCKLAND

If you purchased this book without a cover you should be aware that this book is stolen property. It was reported as "unsold and destroyed" to the publisher, and neither the author nor the publisher has received any payment for this "stripped book."

Recycling programs for this product may not exist in your area.

ISBN-13: 978-0-373-52777-9

SWEET SURRENDER WITH THE MILLIONAIRE

First North American Publication 2010.

Copyright © 2010 by Helen Brooks.

All rights reserved. Except for use in any review, the reproduction or utilization of this work in whole or in part in any form by any electronic, mechanical or other means, now known or hereafter invented, including xerography, photocopying and recording, or in any information storage or retrieval system, is forbidden without the written permission of the publisher, Harlequin Enterprises Limited, 225 Duncan Mill Road, Don Mills, Ontario, Canada M3B 3K9.

This is a work of fiction. Names, characters, places and incidents are either the product of the author's imagination or are used fictitiously, and any resemblance to actual persons, living or dead, business establishments, events or locales is entirely coincidental.

This edition published by arrangement with Harlequin Books S.A.

For questions and comments about the quality of this book please contact us at Customer_eCare@Harlequin.ca.

® and TM are trademarks of the publisher. Trademarks indicated with ® are registered in the United States Patent and Trademark Office, the Canadian Trade Marks Office and in other countries.

www.eHarlequin.com

Printed in U.S.A.

036907369

SWEET SURRENDER WITH THE MILLIONAIRE

CHAPTER ONE

SHE'D done it! It was finally hers. A place where after all the trauma and misery of the last few years she could pull up the drawbridge—metaphorically speaking—and be in her own world. Answerable to no one. No matter it was going to take her years to get the cottage sorted; she could do it at her own pace and it would fill her evenings and weekends, which was just what she wanted. Anyway, if it had been in pristine condition she wouldn't have been able to afford it.

Willow Landon heaved a satisfied sigh and then whirled round and round on the spot before coming dizzily to a halt as she laughed out loud. She was in control of her life again, that was what this cottage meant, and she was *never* going to relinquish that autonomy again.

She gazed round the small empty sitting room, and the peeling wallpaper and dusty floorboards could have been a palace, such was the expression on her rapt face. Walking across to the grimy French doors in which the glass was cracked and the paintwork flaking, she opened them onto the tangled jungle of a garden. Monstrous nettles and brambles confronted her, fighting for supremacy with waist-high weeds and aggressive ivy, which had wound itself over bushes and trees until the whole had become a wall of green. It was impossible to see any grass or paths, but she thought she could spy what looked like an old potting shed in front of the stone wall at the end of what the estate agent had assured her was a quarter of an acre of ground.

She shut her eyes for a moment, imagining it as it would be when she'd finished with it. Roses and honeysuckle climbing the drystone walls, benches and a swinging seat on the smooth green lawn and little arbours she'd create, a fountain running over a stone water feature. She'd cultivate lots of old-fashioned flowers: foxgloves, angelica, lupins, gillyflowers, larkspur, and pinks—*lots* of fragrant pinks and wallflowers and stock. And she'd have her own vegetable plot. But those plans were for the future. For now she'd simply clear the jungle and rake the ground free of the worst of weeds and debris for the winter. The most pressing thing was to get the house in shape, and that would take plenty of elbow grease, patience and money. The first two she had, the third would filter in month by month when she saw what she had left after paying the mortgage and bills.

Her mobile phone rang, and as she fished it out of her jeans pocket and saw the number she sighed inwardly even as she said, 'Hi, Beth,' her tone deliberately bright.

'Willow.' Her name was a reproach. 'I've just phoned the flat and one of the girls told me you moved out today. I can't believe you didn't tell us it was this weekend you're moving. You know Peter and I wanted to help.'

'And I told you that with you being seven months pregnant there was no way. Besides which you're still trying to get straight yourself.' Beth and her husband had only moved from their tiny starter home into a larger three-bedroomed semi two weeks before. 'Anyway, I've had loads of offers of help but it's not necessary. I shall enjoy cleaning and sorting out at my own pace. I've got a bed and a few bits of furniture being delivered this afternoon, but there's so much to do here I don't want to buy much as each room will need completely gutting and the less I have to lug about, the better.'

'But to attempt to move on your *own*.' Beth made it sound as though Willow had gone off to Borneo or outer Mongolia on some hazardous expedition. 'Have you got food in for the weekend?'

Before Willow could reply there was the sound of someone speaking in the background. Then Beth's voice came high and indignant. 'Peter says I'm acting as though you're eight years old instead of twenty-eight. I'm not, am I?'

Willow smiled ruefully. She loved her sister very much and since their parents had been killed in a car crash five years ago they'd become even closer, but she had to admit she was relieved Beth would soon have her baby to fuss over. At thirty, Beth was definitely ready to be a mum. Soothingly—but not absolutely truthfully—she murmured, 'Course not. Look, I've taken some holiday I had owing to get straight. I'll pop in for a chat soon.'

'Great. Come on Monday and stay for dinner,' Beth shot back with alacrity.

Again Willow sighed silently. The planning office in Redditch where she'd worked since leaving university was a stone's throw from Beth's new place, and not far from the house she'd shared with three friends for the last twelve months. The cottage, on the other hand, was an hour's drive away, the last fifteen minutes of which on twisting country lanes. Until she'd got familiar with the journey she would have preferred to drive home while it was still light. Now, in late September, the nights were dropping in. But if she suggested going to see Beth for lunch instead it would mean virtually a whole day's work at the cottage was lost. 'Lovely,' she said dutifully. 'I'll bring dessert but it'll be shop-bought, I'm afraid.'

They talked a little more before Willow excused herself by saying she had a hundred and one things to do, but she didn't immediately get to work. Instead she sank down on the curved stone steps that led from the French doors into the garden. She breathed in the warm morning air, her face uplifted to the sun. Birds twittered in the trees and the sky was a deep cornflower blue. Silly, but she felt nature had conspired with her to give her a break and make moving day as easy as it could be. It was a good start to the rest of her life anyway.

A robin flew down to land on the bottom of the three steps, staring at her for a moment with bright black eyes before darting off. She continued to gaze at the spot where the bird had been, but now her eyes were inward-looking.

This was what the cottage signified: the start of the rest of her life. The past was gone and she couldn't change it or undo the huge mistake she'd made in getting involved with Piers in the first place, but the present and the future were hers now she was free of him. It was up to her to make of them what she would. Just a few months ago she had wanted the world to end; life had lost all colour and each day had been nothing more than a battle to get through before she could take one of the pills the doctor had prescribed and shut off her mind for a little while. But slowly she'd stopped taking the pills to help her sleep, had begun to eat again, been able to concentrate on a TV programme or read a book without her mind returning to Piers and that last terrible night.

She lifted up her slender arms, purposely channelling her mind in a different direction as she stretched and stood up. It had taken time, but she was able to do this now and she was grateful for it. In fact it had probably saved her reason. Whatever, she was herself again—albeit an older, wiser self.

Turning, she went back inside and through the house to the front door. Her trusty little Ford Fiesta was parked on the grass verge at the end of the small front garden, which, like the back, was a tangle of weeds, nettles and briars. The car was packed to the roof with her clothes and personal belongings, along with a box containing cleaning equipment and the new vacuum cleaner she'd bought the day before. She had roughly four hours before her bed and few items of furniture were due to be delivered, and she'd need every minute. The old lady who had lived here before she'd finally been persuaded to move to a nursing home had clearly been struggling for years to cope. The nephew who had overseen her departure from the cottage had apparently cleared it; removing the carpets and curtains—which the estate agent had assured Willow had been falling to pieces—along with everything else. What was left was mountains of dust, dirt and cobwebs, but from what she could see of the grimy floorboards they would be great when stained. And at least she could really put her stamp on things.

Four hours later she'd emptied the vacuum bag umpteen times, but at least the dust from the carpet underlay, which had disintegrated into fine powder, was gone, and most surfaces were relatively clean. The cottage wasn't large, comprising a sitting room, kitchen and bathroom downstairs, and two bedrooms upstairs. There was a kind of scullery attached to the kitchen by means of a door that you opened and stepped down into a six-foot by six-foot bare brick room with a tiny slot of a window, and it was evident the old lady had been in the habit of storing her coal and logs for the fire here. There was no central heating and in the kitchen an ancient range was the only means of cooking. The cottage had been rewired fairly recently though, which was a bonus in view of all the other work she'd need to do, and it had a mains supply of water.

The furniture van arrived and the cheery driver helped Willow manoeuvre her bed and chest of drawers upstairs. There was a built-in wardrobe in the bedroom she'd chosen to sleep in. A two-seater sofa and plumpy armchair and coffee table for the sitting room completed her purchases; her portable TV was in the car, along with her microwave.

That night she fell into bed and was asleep as soon as her head touched the pillow, and for the first time since she had left Piers there were no bad dreams. When Willow awoke in the morning to sunlight streaming in the uncurtained window, she lay for a long time just listening to the birds singing outside and drinking in the peace and solitude. The house she'd shared with her friends for the last months had been on a main road and the traffic noise had filtered in despite the double glazing, but that had been nothing to the noise within most of the time! And before that—

She sat up in bed. She wasn't going to think about the years with Piers in any way, shape or form. New resolution. New start. Off with the old and on with the new. She could *so* do this. She'd always had her fair share of willpower.

The next couple of days were spent cleaning and scrubbing every room, but by the time Willow had dinner with Beth she was satisfied the years of dirt were dealt with. OK, the place needed serious attention, but the roof was sound and she'd keep to her original plan and do a job at a time as the money dictated. Buying furniture had taken every spare penny but she could work on the garden for the rest of her holiday.

She drove home without mishap after an enjoyable evening with Beth and Peter, and the next day began the assault on the garden. By the weekend she was scratched and sore and aching in muscles she hadn't known she had, but she'd cleared a good-sized section of land. Sunday afternoon the sun was still shining and she decided to have a bonfire. That was what people did in the country, after all.

At some time there must have been a small picket fence separating part of the garden. This had long since rotted, but the remains were useful as a base for the bonfire, along with armfuls of other pieces of wood she had found and old newspapers. When she'd opened the door of the dilapidated pottingshed a couple of days earlier, she had found it stacked from floor to ceiling with old newspapers, magazines, cardboard egg boxes and food wrappers. The old lady must have deposited her paper and cardboard there for years before the garden became too overgrown for her to reach it.

Willow piled the brambles and nettles and other vegetation she'd cleared as high as she could. It would take ages to burn the contents of the potting shed alone, but she had until it got dark. She had positioned the bonfire at the end of the garden some feet from the high stone wall. Beyond this, she understood from the estate agent, was the garden of a larger manor house. The house in question was set in extensive grounds and obscured from view by massive old trees, but the landscaped gardens visible from the lane spoke of considerable wealth. It had been the country residence of the local squire who had owned most of the village set in a dip below Willow's cottage in the old days, apparently, and her cottage had been the gatekeeper's property before the cottage and garden had been sold off. These days the manor house was the weekend home of a successful businessman, according to the estate agent.

Once the bonfire was well and truly alight, Willow began to enjoy herself. There was something immensely satisfying in burning all the rubbish and she fetched more piles of newspapers from the potting shed, throwing them into the crackling flames with gay abandon. This would save a good few trips to the local refuse site if nothing else.

Quite when a sense of slowly mounting unease turned into panic, Willow wasn't sure. Her gung-ho approach with the newspapers had resulted in a large quantity of pieces being picked up by the breeze—still merrily burning—and sailing over the wall in ever-increasing numbers. She tried to knock a pile that was smouldering off the fire with a big stick, but only succeeded in fanning the flames.

She had followed a tip of Peter's and drenched the wood at the bottom of the bonfire in petrol before she'd piled the rubbish on it; now there was no stopping the blaze. Increasingly alarmed by the power of the monster she'd created, she retreated to the cottage to fetch a bucket of water to throw on the flames now leaping into the sky with ever-increasing ferocity and strength.

She was still filling the bucket in the kitchen when she heard shouting. Turning off the tap, she picked up the half-full pail and hurried into the garden in time to see the figure of a man hoisting himself astride the stone wall, his curses mingling with the roaring fire and the wild frenzied barking of what sounded like a pack of rabid dogs.

'What the hell are you playing at?' he snarled at her as she approached. 'Have you lost your reason, woman?'

How rude. The abject apology she'd been about to make died on her lips. She stared into a pair of eyes so blue they were dazzling—which wasn't helpful in the circumstances—and stopped dead in her tracks, which caused a good portion of the water in the bucket to slop over onto her grubby work trainers. 'This is my property,' she said coldly. 'And this isn't a smoke-free zone.'

'I've got nothing against the smoke,' he bit back, his tone acid. 'It's your determination to start fires all over the neighborhood I'm objecting to, and the danger to life and limb. One of my dogs has had its fur singed as it is.'

'I'm sorry,' she said, equally acidly.

'You sound it.' He ducked as a particularly large piece of burning paper wafted past his left ear. 'There's bits of this stuff floating in my swimming pool and all over the grounds, and my dogs are playing a game of Russian roulette as we speak. Damp it down, for crying out loud.'

'I was about to when you materialised.'

'With that?' He eyed her bucket with scathing disgust.

'You might as well use an eggcup. Where's your garden hose?'

'I don't have one.' She glared at him, her eyes narrowed.

'Give me strength…'

As he disappeared back into his own garden Willow stared at the spot where he'd been, her cheeks burning, and not wholly because of the heat from the fire, which was intense. What a horrible individual and how dared he growl at her like that? Anyone would think she'd done this on purpose. Couldn't he see it was an accident? She'd hardly meant to send stuff into his stupid garden.

As the breeze mocked her by gathering a handful of paper and causing it to pirouette over the wall she groaned softly. He had a point, of course he had a point, and she would have apologised if he hadn't rushed in all guns blazing. She slung the remaining contents of the bucket on the fire. It treated the paltry amount of water with the contempt it deserved and blazed fiercely as if to confirm she was fighting a losing battle.

She was just about to run back to the house for more water when there was a scrambling noise and the man reappeared. 'Stand back,' he said tersely.

'What?' She stared at him, taken by surprise.

'I said, stand back.' He bent down to someone on his side of the wall as he spoke, adding, 'OK, Jim, I've got it.'

Willow saw the garden hose in his hand a moment before the jet of water hit the flames. For a minute or two all was hissing and spitting and belching smoke, ash from the fire covering her and the surrounding area along with droplets of water. She had instinctively moved when he'd shouted at her, but she was still near enough to the bonfire for the spray to reach her. She stood, utterly taken aback as she watched him douse the flames as though he was enjoying himself. He probably was.

'That's done it.' He passed the hose back to the unseen assistant and turned to look at her. 'Never start a bonfire without having the means at hand to put it out should something like today happen,' he said with what Willow considered sickening righteousness, and then he grinned at her.

She stared at him. The piercing blue eyes were set in a tanned face that was more rugged than handsome and topped by black hair that reached the top of the collar of his open-necked shirt. His smile showed dazzling white teeth and he seemed totally at ease on his perch on the wall now the imminent danger was over. 'Morgan Wright,' he said calmly when she continued to gaze dumbly at him. 'As you may have gathered I'm your next-door neighbour.'

'Willow Landon,' she managed at last, suddenly aware of how she must look as the blue eyes washed over her. 'I—I moved in last week. I've been doing some gardening,' she finished lamely.

He nodded. He was dressed in a blue shirt with the sleeves rolled up and black denim jeans, and his whole appearance was one of strength and virile masculinity. Willow knew she was filthy, her hair bundled up into a ponytail and no make-up on her face. She had never felt at such a disadvantage in the whole of her life. 'I'm sorry about the fire,' she said stiffly after a moment had ticked by, 'but I was about to see to it, like I said.' She took a deep breath and forced herself to add, 'But thank you for your help. I'm sorry to have bothered you.'

His eyes had narrowed slightly at her tone. 'Self-preservation,' he drawled after a moment's silence. 'There's a wooden summer house on my side of the wall and I'd prefer not to see it go up in smoke just yet.'

'I hardly think that would have happened.' She eyed him coolly.

Dark eyebrows rose in a wry quirk. 'Your mother ought to have warned you about being so friendly,' he said, his blue eyes laughing at her. 'Folk could get the wrong impression.'

She knew she was being unreasonable in the circumstances. Unforgivably unreasonable. And she wasn't usually this way. Somehow, though, everything about this man caught her on the raw. She swallowed hard, willing her voice not to falter when she said, 'Thank you again. I'd better start clearing up,' as she turned away, wishing he would disappear as quickly as he'd arrived.

'Want some help?' The deep voice was unforgivably amused.

'No, I can manage.' She didn't look at him as she spoke.

'I've no doubt about that but the offer still stands. Two pair of hands make light work and all that.'

'No, really.' She met the blue gaze again and the impact was like a small electric shock. She felt muscles clench in her stomach as everything in her recoiled from the attraction, but her voice was steady when she said, 'I think I'll go and have a wash and leave the clearing up until tomorrow, actually. Give it a chance to die down completely.'

'Good idea—you don't want to burn yourself.'

Again his eyes were laughing; the covert mockery was galling. Warning herself not to rise to it, Willow pretended to take his words at face value. 'Exactly. Goodbye, Mr Wright.'

'Morgan. We're neighbours, after all.'

She nodded but said nothing, walking back to the cottage and aware all the time of his eyes burning into her back. She didn't look round when she reached the door but she knew he was still sitting on the wall watching her; she could feel it.

Once inside the cottage she leant against the door with her eyes shut for a long moment. Great, just great. What an introduction to her nearest neighbour. Now he would think she was a dizzy female without a brain in her body, which wasn't exactly the sort of impression she wanted to impart to folk hereabouts.

He had been laughing at her the whole time. Well, not the whole time; he had been too angry at first, she amended, opening her eyes with a soft groan. And she hadn't made things any better, going for him like that. But he had been so totally supercilious and aggravating. And that little lecture about having a hose handy when she had a bonfire; how old did he think she was? Still in nursery school?

She levered herself off the door. She was wet and cold and dirty and it was going to take ages to clear up outside tomorrow. She just hoped Mr Know-It-All stayed well clear. If she saw him again for the rest of her life it would be too soon…

CHAPTER TWO

MORGAN waited until the door had closed behind Willow before he jumped down into his garden. He landed beside his gardener-cum-handyman, who eyed him wryly. 'I could be wrong but I got the impression she didn't appreciate your help overmuch.'

'Don't you believe it—she was bowled over by my charm.'

'Oh, aye, you could have fooled me. Pretty, was she?'

Morgan smiled. Jim and his wife, Kitty, had been with him for ten years since he'd moved into the manor house after making his first million or two as a young man of twenty-five. They lived in a large and very comfortable flat above the garage block, and ran his home like clockwork. Kitty was a motherly soul and a wonderful cook and housekeeper. Now in their early sixties, the couple had been unable to have children of their own. Morgan knew they looked on him as the son they'd never had and he, in his turn, was immensely fond of the tall, distinguished-looking man and his small, bustling wife.

'Hard to tell exactly what she did look like under all that dirt,' he said offhandedly, turning and surveying the littered grounds as he added, 'I'll help you start clearing up this lot.'

He thought about what Jim had said, though, as he began to fish pieces of blackened paper out of the swimming pool with the large pool net. Green eyes and red hair, nice combination, and a good figure, but definitely a prickly customer. The way she'd glared at him… He stood for a moment, smiling slightly to himself. It had been a long time since a woman had scowled at him like that; since he'd discovered he had the Midas touch where property was concerned and risen to dizzying heights in the business world they normally fell over backwards to be seen on his arm. There was no vanity in this thought, merely a cynical acknowledgement of the power of money.

Beginning work again, he pictured her in his mind's eye. There had been a nicely rounded, firm little *derrière* in those jeans as she'd marched away down the garden, her silky red ponytail swinging in indignation.

To Morgan's surprise, he felt a certain part of his anatomy respond to the memory, becoming as hard as a rock. In answer to his body's reaction, he said out loud, 'She's too young.' She didn't look a day over twenty, all bright-eyed and bushy-tailed. He preferred his women to be sophisticated and worldly-wise, happy to be shown a good time but without any delusions of till-death-us-do-part and *definitely* charming, easy company. He worked hard and played hard and he was sufficiently wealthy to do both on his terms.

His mouth hardened, although he was unaware of it. When he had first entered the business world he'd been taken for a ride once or twice, but it had been valuable experience and he'd learnt from it. Very quickly he'd understood he couldn't afford to take anyone or anything at face value. The same applied to his love life. At twenty-four, just before he'd hit the big time, he'd met Stephanie. Stephanie Collins. Blonde, bright, beautiful. When they began dating he thought he was the luckiest man in the world but after six months she'd sent him a typical 'Dear John' letter and disappeared into the blue yonder with a balding, wrinkled millionaire. Ironic, really, because if she'd waited a year or so he could have given her everything she'd ever wanted and without being pawed over by a man old enough to be her grandfather. But, again, the episode had taught him plenty for which he was grateful.

He nodded mentally to the thought. In fact the Stephanie thing had woken him up to the fact that the whole for-ever scenario wasn't for him. His parents having been killed in a car crash when he was just a baby, he'd been shunted round various relatives until he'd gone away to university at the age of eighteen. From that point he'd made his own way in the world, but until Stephanie he hadn't faced the need he had of belonging to someone, of putting down roots and having a home that was his. The need had made him realise he was vulnerable and he hadn't liked that.

Morgan straightened and threw the net to one side. No, he hadn't liked that at all. But then the money had started to roll in. He had been able to buy this place and also a chrome and glass one-bedroomed apartment in London where he stayed weekdays. And nowadays all he required of his women was honesty, which was why he made a point of only dating successful career women who were as autonomous as he was. And he was satisfied with that. His square chin came up, thrusting slightly forward as though someone had challenged him on the statement.

One of the dogs pushed its nose into his hand and he didn't have to look down to see who it was. Bella had been the first of the German Shepherds he'd bought a couple of years after acquiring the manor house and she was still his favourite. As a puppy she'd had a weak stomach and been prone to vomiting attacks that could swiftly put her life at risk; many a time he'd sat up all night giving her sips of a rehydrating formula prescribed by the local vet. Maybe it was that that had created the special bond between them. She had grown into a strong, beautiful animal who was as intelligent as she was gentle, but in spite of her sweet temper she was the undisputed leader of his five dogs. And she always knew when he was disturbed about something or other.

'I'm all right, girl.' He looked down into the trusting brown eyes. 'Thinking a bit too much, maybe, that's all.' He glanced over to where Jim was still picking up fragments of charred paper, his progress hampered by the other four dogs who were chasing bits here and there. Then his gaze moved over the beautifully tended grounds until it rested on the fine old house in the distance, the mellow stone and mullioned windows set off perfectly by the exquisitely thatched roof.

He was a lucky man. He nodded mentally to the thought. Answerable to no one and in complete control of every aspect of his life. And that was the way things would stay. Snapping his fingers at Bella, he made his way to the house, the dog following at his heels as she always did, given half a chance.

Kitty looked up from rolling pastry as he walked into the kitchen, her round, homely face enquiring. 'Put the fire out, did you?' she said, asking the obvious. 'What was the lass thinking of to do that? I hope you read her the Riot Act—she could have had the roof on fire. Bit simple, is she?'

Ridiculously he didn't like that. Remembering the spark in the green eyes, he said quietly, 'Far from it. She struck me as impetuous, that's all.'

'Oh, aye?' Kitty was a northerner and always spoke her mind. 'Plain daft, I'd call it. Still, let's hope she's learnt her lesson.'

Morgan wondered why he was feeling defensive on the girl's behalf when she'd behaved so foolishly. With Bella following he walked through to the drawing room at the front of the house, the windows of which overlooked wide sweeping lawns and manicured flowerbeds. Pouring himself a whisky from the cocktail cabinet in a corner of the room, he flung himself into a chair and switched on the massive TV with the remote. An inane quiz show came on the screen and after channel-hopping for a while he turned the TV off, drained his glass and made his way to his study.

The room was masculine and without frills, a floor-to-ceiling bookcase occupying one wall and his massive Edwardian twin-pedestal desk dominating the space. The study could appear cosy in the winter when Kitty saw to it a good fire was kept burning in the large ornate grate, but now the room merely had the air of being functional. He sat down at the desk.

Morgan gazed musingly at the tooled-leather writing surface without reaching for the stack of files he'd brought back to work on. When he'd got home at the weekend Kitty had been full of the news the village grapevine had passed on. A woman had bought Keeper's Cottage and was living in it alone, and to date she'd had no visitors. He hadn't been particularly interested; if he'd thought about it at all he'd probably jumped to the conclusion the woman in question was a middle-aged or retired individual who wanted a bit of peace and quiet from the hurly-burly of modern-day living.

He raised his head, his eyes taking in the tiny dancing particles of dust the slanting sunshine through the window had caught in its beam.

But the occupant of Keeper's Cottage was far from being old. The woman who had glared at him with such hostility was very young and attractive and clearly had a mind of her own, which begged the question—why had she chosen to live in such seclusion? Did she work? And if so, where? Who was Willow Landon and why didn't she like men? Or perhaps it was *him*, rather than the whole male gender, she didn't like?

This thought caused his firm, sensual mouth to tighten and he leaned back in the big leather chair for a moment, drumming his fingers on the padded arms.

This was crazy. Annoyance with himself brought him reaching abruptly for a file. It didn't matter who Willow Landon was or what had brought her to this neck of the woods. He'd probably never talk to the woman again; in all the time he'd lived here he had made a point of not becoming friendly with the neighbours. This was his bolt hole, the place where he could be himself and to hell with the rest of the world. His London apartment was where he socialised and conducted out-of-hours business affairs—other affairs too, come to it.

Morgan opened the file, scanning the papers inside but without really taking them in. He had ended his latest liaison the week before. Charmaine had been a delightful companion and—being a high-grade lawyer with nerves of steel and keenly intelligent—she was at the top of her profession and much sought after. Only he hadn't realised she thought it perfectly acceptable to endow her favours to other men on the occasions she wasn't seeing him. Unfashionable, perhaps, but he had always had an aversion to polygamy and he had told her so, as he'd thought quite reasonably.

Charmaine had called him pharisaical after throwing her cocktail in his face. What was the difference, she'd hissed, in sleeping with other men before and after an affair, and not during? They both knew they didn't want a for-ever scenario, and they had fun together and the sex was great; why couldn't he just go with the flow and enjoy it? Other men did.

He had looked into her beautiful, angry face and known any desire he'd had for the perfectly honed female body in front of him had gone. He didn't want to go where someone else had been the night before; it was as simple as that. He gave and expected fidelity for as long as a relationship lasted, and he couldn't operate any other way. The scene that had followed had been ugly.

Smiling grimly to himself, Morgan cleared his mind of anything but the Thorpe account in front of him. He needed to check the figures very carefully because something hadn't sat right with him when he'd glanced at them at the office. He had found his gut instinct rarely failed him.

Sure enough, a few minutes later he found a couple of discrepancies that were enough to raise question marks in his mind about the takeover that was being proposed. He'd have to go into things more thoroughly once he was back in the office, he decided, slinging the file aside and raking his hand through his hair.

The movement brought the faint smell of woodsmoke into his nostrils and he frowned, his earlier thoughts taking hold. Women were a necessary indulgence but they were a breed apart, and Charmaine had reminded him of the fact. Not that he'd needed much reminding. And that applied to all women—angry, green-eyed redheads included. She certainly had a temper to go with the hair, that was for sure. His mouth twisted in a smile. Not that he minded spirit in a woman. It often made life interesting. He'd never understood men who liked their women to be subservient shadows, scared to say boo to a goose.

He stretched his long legs, reaching for another file and feeling faintly annoyed at how he'd allowed himself to become distracted. Within moments he was engrossed in the papers in front of him and everything else had vanished from his mind, but the faint scent of woodsmoke still hung in the air.

CHAPTER THREE

'HOW *embarrassing*. Poor you.' In spite of her words Beth's tone was more eager than sympathetic and her face was alight with interest. 'And this guy who owns the place, he must be worth a bit if the manor house is just his weekend home?'

'I've got no idea how wealthy he is or isn't.'

'Is he young or old? I mean, grey-haired or what?'

'What's his age got to do with anything?' Willow found she was regretting mentioning the episode at the weekend to her sister now. She had called in for a coffee and quick chat after work mainly, she had to admit, because she was still smarting from Morgan Wright's condemnation and wanted someone to commiserate with her. She might have known Beth wouldn't play ball.

Beth shrugged. 'I just wondered if he was tasty, that's all.'

Willow had to smile. 'He's a man, Beth. Not a toasted sandwich.'

'Is he, though?' Beth had got the bit between her teeth.

'Is he what?' said Willow, deliberately prevaricating.

'Fanciable.' Beth grinned at her. 'Hunky, you know.'

She was *so* not going to do this. 'I didn't notice, added to which he's more likely than not married. Attractive, wealthy men of a certain age tend to be snapped up pretty fast.'

'So he *is* tasty?' Beth sat forward interestedly.

Willow changed the subject in the one way that couldn't fail. 'So you've finished the nursery now, then? Can I take a look?'

She oohed and ahhed at the pretty lemon and white room, which already had more fluffy toys than any one child could ever want, along with a wardrobe full of tiny little vests and socks and Babygros, and then made her escape before Beth returned to their previous conversation. Her sister rarely let anything drop before she was completely satisfied.

The weather had broken at the beginning of the week and it had got progressively colder day by day. Today, Friday, was the first of October and the month had announced its intentions with a biting wind and rain showers. It started to rain again when she was halfway home, but this was no shower, just a steady downpour that had her scurrying out of the car and into the house in record speed once she was home.

After several days of battling with the Aga cooker she'd finally got the knack of persuading it into action just before she'd resumed work, but she hadn't lit it all week, making do with microwave meals. She could imagine the kitchen was a warm, cosy place with the range in action, but each evening she'd lit a fire in the sitting-room grate and sat hunched over it for the first hour until the chill had been taken off the room.

Putting a match to the fire she had laid that morning before she'd left for work, she walked through into the kitchen to switch the electric kettle on, shivering as she went. The last few days had pointed out her main priority was to get oil-fired central heating installed in the cottage as quickly as she could; the sitting-room fire would be a nice feature to keep but was woefully inadequate as the sole means of warmth.

Once she was nursing a hot mug of coffee she returned to the sitting room and threw a couple more logs and a few extra pieces of coal on the fledgling flames, fixing the guard round the fire before she went upstairs to change into jeans and a warm jumper. That done, and in spite of the fact the room was freezing, she sat for some time on the bed sipping the coffee as she stared at her reflection in the long thin mirror on the opposite wall, her mind a million miles away.

It had been a tiring week at work with several minor panics and she was still getting used to the long drive home, but it wasn't that that occupied her thoughts, but how her life had changed in the last twelve months and especially in the two weeks since she had moved into the cottage. OK, it might be pretty basic right now but it was *hers*. She had done this on her own. Why hadn't she had the courage to leave Piers long before she had done and make a new life without him? Why had she tried and tried and tried to make the marriage work long after she had known she'd married a monster? A handsome, charming, honey-tongued monster who had fooled her as completely as he did everyone else. At first. Until she'd tied the knot.

Why? a separate part of her mind answered. You know why.

Yes, she did. She nodded her acquiescence. Piers had been the master of mind games and he had moulded and manipulated her to his will so subtly she hadn't been aware of his power over her until it was too late. He had convinced her she was worthless, useless, that she couldn't manage without him, and she had believed him utterly. Because she'd trusted him, fool that she was.

Rising abruptly, she walked closer to the mirror and stared into the slanted green eyes looking back at her. What had attracted Piers to her that night nearly six years ago? There'd been other, prettier girls in the nightclub. But he'd chosen her and she'd been thrilled, falling head over heels in love with him from the first date. Seven months later her parents had been killed and when he'd asked her to marry him just after the funeral she'd accepted at once, needing his love and comfort to combat the pain and grief. A month later they were Mr and Mrs Piers Gregory. And she had been caught in a trap.

Marry in haste, repent at leisure. An older, wiser friend had murmured that to her when she had announced her wedding date but at the time she'd been too much in love and too heartbroken about her parents to take heed to the warning.

Shaking her head at the naive girl she had been then, Willow made her way downstairs. On entering the sitting room she was slightly alarmed by the roaring fire, although it had warmed the room up nicely. Hastily banking down the flames with some damp slack, she walked through to the kitchen and made herself another coffee. Give it a few minutes and she'd toast the crumpets she'd bought for her tea in front of the fire once it was glowing red; there was nothing nicer than toasted crumpets with lashings of butter. And this was definitely a comfort night.

She had just picked up the mug of coffee when a sharp pounding on her front door almost made her drop it. Her nerves jangling, she hurried into the tiny hall and opened the door, her eyes widening as she took in the tall dark man in front of her. And he looked just as angry as when she'd first seen him.

'Are you aware your chimney's on fire?' Morgan said grimly.

'What?' She stared at him. 'What are you talking about?'

'Look.' To her amazement she found herself hauled forward by a hard hand on her arm as he pointed to the roof of the cottage. Massive flames were lighting the night sky.

Wrenching herself free, Willow stared aghast at the chimney. Never having lived in a house that accommodated coal fires, she'd had no idea a chimney could catch fire.

'I've called the fire brigade and they should be here shortly.' Even as he spoke the sound of a siren in the distance could be heard coming rapidly nearer.

'You called the fire brigade?' Willow echoed in horror. 'Can't it just go out? I won't put any more coal on.'

'Are you serious?' Morgan stared at her through the rain, which had settled down to a fine drizzle. 'You could lose the whole cottage. The chimney is on *fire*, for pity's sake.'

'But a chimney is supposed to have smoke and flames go up it,' she answered sharply. 'That's what they do.'

'Up it, yes. If it catches fire that's a whole different ball game. Did you have it swept before you lit the first fire?'

'Swept?' He could have been talking double Dutch.

'Give me strength.'

He shut his eyes for a moment in a manner that made Willow want to kick him, but then the fire engine had screeched to a halt and in the ensuing pandemonium she forgot about Morgan.

Half an hour later the fire engine and the very nice firemen left and Willow stood staring at the devastation in her sitting room. She was barely aware of Morgan at the side of her until he murmured, 'What is it with you and fire anyway?'

She wanted to come back at him with a cutting retort, but she knew if she tried to speak she would cry. Swallowing hard, she picked her way across the wet, sooty floor and reached for the photograph of her parents on the mantelpiece. Wiping the black spots off the glass, she held the photograph to her when she turned to face him. 'Thank—thank you for calling the fire brigade.' The fireman had said she'd been minutes away from having a major catastrophe on her hands. 'I want to start cleaning up now, so if you don't mind...'

He didn't take the hint. 'I'll help you mop up the worst and then I suggest you leave the main clearing up till tomorrow. Nothing will seem so bad after a good night's sleep and a hearty breakfast.'

Willow stared round the room and her expression must have spoken volumes because Morgan smiled the lopsided grin that she'd registered the first time she had met him before saying wryly, 'OK, it might, but this'll take hours and it'll be better in daylight.' He shivered, adding, 'Haven't you any heating in this place? It's as cold in here as it is outside.'

Willow's eyes went involuntarily to the blackened fireplace.

'No central heating? No storage heaters or fan heaters?'

She shook her head. 'Not yet, but I will do something soon.'

'OK, this is what we do,' he said after a moment's

silence. 'We mop up like I said and then you're coming home with me for a hot meal and a bath before you spend the night at my place. I'll bring you back in the morning and we'll tackle the cleaning then. At least you'll be in a better frame of mind to cope.'

Was he mad? Adrenalin surged in a welcome flood, enabling her to straighten and say steadily, 'Thank you, Mr Wright, but that's really not necessary. I can manage perfectly well.'

'I've seen the results of you managing…twice.'

Willow's chin raised a notch. 'Thank you,' she said for the third time, her voice thin, 'but I'd like to be on my own now. I'm not a child so please don't treat me like one.'

She saw the amazingly blue eyes narrow in irritation. 'Are you always this stubborn?'

The smell of soot was thick in her nostrils and she was so cold her fingers were numb. All she wanted was for him to leave so she could sit down and howl. 'Please go,' she said weakly.

It was like talking to a brick wall. Somehow in the next few minutes she found herself covering the floorboards with a thick layer of newspapers—Morgan had fetched these from the potting shed and to his credit he didn't make any comment whatsoever—before fetching her handbag and coat and locking the front door of the cottage. She felt shivery and shaky and it was just easier to comply rather than argue, besides which she was cold and hungry and the thought of tackling the cleaning-up process tonight was unbearable.

It wasn't until Willow reached the rickety garden gate that she noticed the Harley-Davidson parked down the lane on the grass verge. As Morgan walked over to the powerful machine she stopped dead. 'That's yours? You came on that?'

'Yep.' She could see his blue eyes glittering in the deep shadows as he turned and smiled. 'When I saw the flames I figured I'd better get round here as fast as I could.'

She waved her hand helplessly. 'But you live next door.'

'A minute or two can make all the difference with fire. I didn't know whether I was going to have to pull you out of a burning house at that stage.' He shrugged. 'It can happen.'

He started the engine and the quiet of the night was rudely shattered as he drove to her gate. 'Get on.'

She had already noticed that he was even taller than she had thought him to be when he was perched on the wall. Morgan Wright was big, very big, and it was muscled strength that padded his shoulders and chest. In fact he gave off an aura of strength from his face—which was rugged with sharply defined planes and angles and no softness—to his feet, which were encased in black leather boots. The thought of clambering up on the bike and holding onto the hard male body was blushingly intimate, but she could hardly walk beside him. She had no choice but to agree.

Blessing the fact she had changed from her pencil-thin office skirt to jeans, Willow slid onto the bike, her handbag over one shoulder. Morgan wasn't wearing a coat, just jeans and a shirt, and as she put her arms round his waist the warmth of his body flowed through her fingers. She felt him jerk.

'Hell, you're like a block of ice,' he muttered.

Funnily enough, she was aware of that herself. 'Sorry.'

There was no chance to say anything more before they roared off. After some two hundred yards Morgan turned into his own grounds through open six-foot wrought-iron gates. The drive wound through mature trees and bushes, which hid the house from the road, but then a bowling-green-smooth lawn came into view and the manor house was in front of them. It was quite stunning.

The motorbike drew to a halt at the bottom of wide semicircular stone steps, which led to a massive studded front door that could have graced a castle. Willow could hear dogs barking from within the house and they sounded ferocious.

'Are you OK with dogs?' Morgan asked as he helped her off the Harley. 'There's a few of them so be prepared.'

'If they're OK with me,' she said more weakly than she would have liked. 'And I prefer they don't look on me as food.'

He grinned. 'They've already been fed for the night.'

'That's comforting.'

He took her arm, leading her up the steps. 'My housekeeper and her husband will be back shortly—they're visiting a friend in hospital—and dinner'll be about eight, but that'll give you time for a long hot soak. You're shaking with cold.'

Willow was glad he was already opening the door and she didn't have to reply. For the life of her she couldn't have said if it was the icy night air making her tremble or the enforced intimacy with the very male man at her side. And he smelt delicious, the sort of delicious that would cost a small fortune for a few mls and definitely came courtesy of a designer label.

Contrary to what she had expected the dogs didn't come at them pell-mell but in an orderly group that sat at their feet without any jostling. 'I'll introduce you and you can give the obligatory pat—that way they'll know you're a friend and off the menu. They never eat my friends.'

Morgan's lazy tone and the laughter in his eyes informed her he was well aware of her unease and enjoying it. Willow looked at him coldly. She didn't know why but everything about Morgan Wright irritated her, ungrateful though that was in the circumstances. Criminally ungrateful, to be truthful.

Introductions finished, the pack padded off led by the large female called Bella, much to Willow's relief. It wasn't that she disliked dogs but she'd never had anything to do with them, either as a child or an adult. Her mother had been allergic to most types of pet hair and although she and Beth had had a hamster each, which they had kept in their bedrooms, it wasn't the same as an animal free to roam like these dogs. And they were so big, especially their jaws. In fact they resembled wolves more than pet dogs, in her opinion. She gazed after them, her eyes taking in the luxury of her surroundings from the pale wood floor to the beautiful paintings adorning the cream walls in the massive hall. Everything was perfect.

She suddenly became aware that Morgan was looking at her with unconcealed appraisal. 'Freckles,' he said, as though that made up the sum total of her appearance. 'Lots of them.'

She inwardly winced. The hundreds of freckles that covered most of her creamy skin had been the bane of her life from when she was first teased about them at nursery school. Reminding herself that he was going the extra mile in being neighbourly and that he had probably saved her cottage—if not her life—this night, she forced herself to smile and say, 'Goes with the hair, I'm afraid. But you learn to live with what you can't change.'

'You don't like them? I do.' He continued to study her.

If he were covered in an infinity of them he might think differently. Willow shrugged. 'There's worse things to contend with than freckles.' Much worse.

His gaze hadn't left her face. 'And your eyes are truly green without a fleck of brown. Unusual.'

She wasn't about to stand there like a lemon submitting to his scrutiny. Moving past him, she looked to where a magnificent winding staircase led to a galleried first floor. 'This is a beautiful house. How long have you lived here?'

'Just over ten years.' It was as if she had reminded him to play the host as he added, 'Can I get you a drink or would you like that bath first? Or both, come to it.'

'The bath, please.' The bright lighting in the hall had brought an awareness that her jeans and jumper were covered in soot and she must look like something the cat had dragged in. Morgan's jeans and shirt were bearing evidence of the events of the evening too. Somehow, though, he still looked good.

'I think I'll join you.' As her eyes shot to meet his a dawning mockery in the blue gaze made it clear that he knew the conclusion she'd jumped to. 'Not literally, of course,' he added smoothly. 'You in your bath and me in mine.'

The second bane of her life, which again went with the red hair, rushed in on a tide of crimson. She didn't blush quite so readily these days but this one was a corker and she knew it. 'Of course,' she managed with a coolness that was rendered null and void by her beetroot face. 'What else?'

'What else indeed.' He smiled gently.

Hateful man. OK, he might have the good Samaritan thing down to a fine art, but he hadn't stopped laughing at her since the first moment they'd met, except when he was yelling insults, that was. He'd already made it quite clear he thought she was the original hare-brained female, and she wasn't. She *wasn't.* She had survived a destructive marriage and built a new life for herself, and that alone merited enough Brownie points to fill the ocean. Several oceans on several planets.

'I'll show you your room.' Morgan's voice was pleasant and Willow nodded her head with what she hoped was dignified hauteur. She thought she saw his lips twist, but maybe not.

He stood aside for her to precede him when they reached the staircase, and she found she had almost forgotten how to walk as she climbed the stairs. Her jeans were old and had shrunk to fit her body like a comfortable second skin, but it didn't feel so comfortable with the laser-like blue eyes behind her. The old adage of 'does my bum look big in this?' was at the forefront of her mind with each step. It didn't make for easy walking.

When they reached the wide gracious landing Morgan led her to the first door on their left, pausing and opening it before he said, 'You should find everything you need in the en-suite and there's a robe and slippers in the wardrobe.'

'Thank you.' She smiled politely. 'You're very kind.'

'See you downstairs later for that drink.'

She nodded, fairly scuttling into the bedroom and shutting the door behind her. Only then did she let out her breath in a long sigh. She'd been mad to come here; whatever had possessed her? She didn't do things like this. She had always envied people who acted impulsively and took risks, knowing she was the exact opposite herself. Not that spending the night at a neighbour's house in such circumstances was exactly a risk…

A mental image of Morgan Wright came to mind and she groaned softly. Or it wouldn't be if the neighbour in question were any other than Morgan. But no, she was being silly. What did she think he was going to do, for goodness' sake? Steal into her bedroom and have his wicked way with her like the villain in an old black and white movie? He'd offered her a bed and a hot meal for the night, that was all, and she ought to be grateful. She *was* grateful, but she wished he weren't so…

Her mind couldn't quite categorise what Morgan Wright was, and after a couple of moments she gave up the attempt and walked further into the room. It was gorgeous—large and airy and decorated in soft shades of silver and cream, with touches of dark chocolate in the bed-coverings and curtains. The en-suite was equally impressive, the chocolate marble bath sunk into the floor with elegant silver fittings and the massive shower at the other end of the bathroom large enough for a rugby team. A profusion of soft fluffy towels were stored on glass shelves, along with toiletries of every description. Willow even noticed two new toothbrushes and a tube of toothpaste. The two basins, toilet and bidet were all in chocolate marble but the tiled floor, walls and ceiling, along with the bath-linen, were the same light cream as the bedroom. And this was just a guest room!

Willow stared at her reflection in the mirror that took up half of one wall opposite the bath. And groaned again.

Five minutes later she lay luxuriating in expensive foamy bubbles, tense muscles slowly beginning to relax as the hot water did its job. Her toes didn't reach the end of the bath and the marble had been formed to provide a natural pillow for the occupant's head; she felt she could stay in it all night.

She roused herself at one point to wash her hair, but then slid under the water to her neck again for a last indulgent soak, and she was like that when a knock came at the bathroom door. Shooting to her feet so quickly she sent a wave of water washing onto the floor, she grabbed a bath towel and wrapped it round her as she said, 'Yes? What is it?'

'It's Kitty, dear. Morgan's housekeeper. Just to say I've done my best with your clothes for now, but if you want to leave them outside your door when you go to bed tonight I'll have them laundered for you in the morning so they're nice and fresh.'

'Oh, no, no, that's all right.' Willow stepped out of the bath and made her way to the door, opening it as she said, 'Please, they'll be fine till I get home tomorrow morning,' to the small, smiling woman waiting outside. 'I feel bad enough arriving unannounced for dinner as it is. I'm so sorry.'

'Go on with you.' Kitty flapped her hand. 'I'm just glad Morgan had the sense to invite you after what happened. Men don't always think on their feet, do they?' She winked conspiratorially.

'I guess not.' Actually she suspected Morgan would.

'Still, all's well that ends well. I can give you the name of the chimney sweep we use if that's any help? Nice lad, he is, and he makes a good clean job of it. Doesn't charge the earth either.'

Willow smiled ruefully into the round little face. 'If you could see the state of my cottage right now a bit of dust and soot from a chimney sweep would be nothing. I…I feel so stupid. You must all think I haven't got the sense I was born with.'

Kitty, who had been airing her views on the ineptitude of 'city' dwellers to her husband for the last twenty minutes, clicked her tongue. 'Not a bit of it, lass. How were you to know the chimney needed sweeping? I blame the estate agent—they should point out these things as part of their job. Quick enough to take their cut, aren't they? But that's typical of today's generation. There's no pride in a job well done any more, more's the pity. People do as much as they can get away with.'

'I hope you're not including me in that statement.'

As the dark smoky voice preceded Morgan strolling into the bedroom through the door Kitty had left open Willow's hands tightened instinctively round the bath sheet. For a moment she had the mad impulse to step back and shut the bathroom door but she controlled it—just. Her eyes wide, she stared at him.

Morgan had changed into a fresh shirt and jeans and his damp hair was slicked back from his face. The five o'clock shadow she had noticed earlier was gone too. Ridiculously the thought of him shaving to have dinner with her caused her stomach to tighten, even as she told herself he probably always shaved twice a day. His open-necked grey shirt showed the springy black hair of his chest and his black jeans were tight across the hips. Every nerve in her body was sensitised, much to her aggravation.

He seemed faintly surprised to see her still wrapped in a bath towel, his voice soft as he drawled, 'Not ready yet, then.'

'No, I— No. No, not yet.' Oh, for goodness' sake, pull yourself together, girl, she told herself angrily, annoyed at her stammering. You're perfectly decent. Only the look in his eyes hadn't made her feel that way. Even more alarming, she had liked the warm approval turning the blue of his eyes to deep indigo. For the first time in a long while she'd felt...womanly.

'We'd better leave you to get ready.' Kitty took charge, her voice suddenly brisk. 'Dinner's at eight, dear. All right? And there's a hairdryer in the top drawer of the dressing table.'

As the little woman bustled off Morgan smiled a lazy smile. 'Red or white?' he asked softly, the words almost a caress.

'Sorry?' She hoped she didn't look as vacant as she sounded.

'The wine with our meal. Red or white?'

Her hair was dripping over her face and all she wanted was to end this conversation and put a door between them. 'Red, please.' Actually she didn't mind but she wasn't going to say that.

One eyebrow lifted. 'Funny. I'd got you down as a white-wine girl,' he said easily.

In spite of herself she couldn't resist asking, 'Oh, yes? Why?' even as she mentally kicked herself for giving him the opportunity for more mockery. As if he needed an opportunity!

He shrugged. 'Girls of a certain age seem to go for white wine.' He smiled charmingly. 'Or that's what I've found.'

Did they indeed? And of course a man like Morgan Wright would know. The green eyes he'd spoke about narrowed. 'What age is that?' she asked evenly, determined to show no reaction.

'Twenty, twenty-one.'

Willow didn't know whether to feel pleased or insulted. If he was judging her age purely on her appearance, then that was fine, but if this was another way of saying she was silly and immature… Warily, she said, 'It's my twenty-ninth birthday in a few weeks.' And make of that what you will.

'You're joking.' He let his gaze travel over her body, top to toes. 'It's obviously a gene thing.'

It was actually. Beth looked years younger than she was and their mother had often been taken as their older sister. She nodded. 'Advantage as one gets older but definitely irritating when you're asked for ID at a nightclub,' she said as coolly as she could considering her face had decided to explode with colour again.

He didn't seem to notice her discomfiture. 'Never had that problem myself,' he said with a crooked smile. 'I think I was born looking twenty-one.'

Willow could believe it. Morgan Wright was one of those men who made it impossible to imagine him as a child. The flagrant masculinity was so raw, so tough and virile she couldn't envisage him as a vulnerable little boy. She shivered although she wasn't cold.

'Sorry, this is undoing all the good work the hot bath's done. You get dressed and I'll see you downstairs. The sitting room is to your right once you're in the hall, incidentally.' He had turned as he spoke, and, having reached the bedroom door, shut it quietly behind him.

Willow stared after him for a few moments before she pulled herself together. She found the hairdryer Kitty had spoken of and dried her hair so it fell in a sleek curtain framing her face. She was lucky with her hair. Thick and silky, it was no trouble as long as she had a good cut.

Grimacing, she dressed in her grubby jeans and jumper, although thanks to Kitty's ministrations they were more presentable than when she'd arrived. Fishing out the odd bits of make-up she always kept in her handbag for an emergency, she applied eyeshadow and mascara before finishing with lip gloss. The result wasn't spectacular but better, and better was good considering this man always seemed to see her when she looked as if she'd been pulled through a hedge backwards.

She stopped titivating and stared into the green eyes in the mirror. He must think she was some kind of nutcase and she hadn't done much to convince him otherwise. Perhaps she *was* a nutcase, at that. At uni she'd always been one of the more restrained ones, looking on with a mixture of embarrassment and envy when some of her more wild friends had gone skinny-dipping on a day out by the river or related their antics at the latest wild party they'd attended. But now they were all lawyers or doctors or 'something' in the fashion industry, and a few had successful marriages to boot. Whereas she…

This train of thought was too depressing to follow, besides which it was two minutes to eight. Taking a deep breath, Willow smoothed her jeans over her hips, trying to ignore the sooty smell, and smiled at the face in the mirror. 'You're going to be fine. He's a man, just a man, and this is one night out of the rest of your life. It isn't a big deal so don't make it one.'

And talking to yourself was the first sign of madness.

CHAPTER FOUR

MORGAN WRIGHT wasn't a man given to second-guessing himself. In fact he'd built his small empire by going for the jugular and to hell with it if he'd got it wrong—which, it must be said, he rarely did. He was at the top of his game professionally and comfortingly satisfied with life in general. So why, he asked himself as he sat absently ruffling the fur on Bella's head, the rest of the dogs piled round his feet, was he regretting inviting Willow to stay the night? It didn't make sense.

A muscle knotted in his cheek and he swallowed the last of the Negroni he'd made for himself after coming downstairs. The bittersweet cocktail was one of his favourites and he usually took his time and enjoyed it in a leisurely way, but tonight the mix of Campari, sweet vermouth and gin barely registered on his taste buds. He was all at odds with himself and he didn't like it.

He set the squat, straight-sided glass he always used for his pre-dinner cocktails on the small table beside him, frowning. He would have bet his bottom dollar she was no older than twenty, but if she was to be believed you could add practically another decade to that. And he didn't doubt her. What woman would add years to her age, after all? No, she was nearly twenty-nine.

He raked back a quiff of hair that persisted in falling over his forehead, and the restrained irritation in the action brought Bella's eyes to his face as she whined softly.

'It's all right, girl.' He patted the noble head reassuringly even as a separate part of his mind asked the question, but was it? He didn't like the way his new neighbour made him feel, that was it in a nutshell. He was way past the sweaty palms and uncontrollable urges stage, damn it. That had died a death after Stephanie and since then he'd made sure his head was in full control of his heart and the rest of him. He had a couple of friends who'd let their hearts rule their heads and both of them were paying for it in hefty alimony payments and only seeing their kids every other weekend—if they were lucky. Women were another species, that was the truth of it. Love, if it even existed, was too fragile a thing to trust in, too weighted with possible pitfalls. Like another wealthier, more successful patsy coming along.

Knowing his thinking was flawed, he rose abruptly from his seat and walked across the room to stand looking out over his grounds. OK, there were men and women who loved each other for a lifetime—maybe. But how many of these 'perfect' relationships were for real? How many merely papered over the cracks for reasons of their own? Thousands, millions.

'Ten minutes to dinner.'

Kitty interrupted his thoughts and as he swung round and nodded it was as though the small, plump woman standing in the doorway was a challenge to his thoughts. He couldn't doubt the strength and authenticity of what Jim and Kitty had, but they were the exception that proved the rule. There were hundreds of millions of men and women in the world; you had more chances of winning the lottery than finding what the women's magazines called a soulmate.

'The lass not down yet?' Kitty asked cheerily.

'No, not yet.' He hoped she'd take the hint and disappear.

Kitty came further into the room, her voice dropping as she murmured, 'I wonder what's made a young lass like that buy Keeper's Cottage? Someone of her age should be sharing a flat with friends and having fun. Tisn't right to bury yourself away like she's done.'

His voice dry, Morgan said, 'She's older than she looks.'

'Oh, aye?' Kitty nodded. 'That makes more sense. How old is she, then?'

'Nearly twenty-nine,' Morgan said expressionlessly.

'Is that so?' Kitty nodded again. 'Fancy that.'

Morgan grinned. Kitty was trying very hard to appear nonchalant but he could see the matchmaking gleam in her eye. The little woman had been on a mission to find a 'nice' wife for him for years; it was an irresistible challenge to her despite knowing his views on the subject. Walking across to her, he gently tucked a strand of grey hair behind her ear as he murmured softly, 'Forget it, Kitty. Between you and me Miss Willow Landon doesn't like me very much so there's no hope in that direction, OK?'

It clearly wasn't. Visibly bristling, Kitty stared at him. 'I don't see why after the way you've helped her.'

'Personality clash,' he said briefly. 'That's all.'

'Personality clash? And what's that when it's at home?'

Wishing he'd kept his mouth shut, Morgan took a deep

breath, then let it out. 'She's been polite and grateful so don't get on your high horse, woman. I just meant I'm clearly not her type any more than she's mine.'

A slight noise in the doorway brought their heads turning. Willow was standing there and he suspected she'd heard his last remark from the colour in her cheeks. As if that weren't enough the sight of her—hair falling to her shoulders in silken strands, eyes as green as emeralds and her soft, half-open mouth—sent a jolt of desire sizzling through his veins. Mentally cursing Kitty and her matchmaking and not least the primal urges this young red-haired woman seemed able to inspire so easily, Morgan decided prevarication wasn't an option. As Kitty beat a hasty retreat he said quietly, 'Sorry, you obviously weren't supposed to hear that.'

'Obviously.' The green eyes were as cold as glass.

Damn it. Following the line that honesty was the best policy, Morgan shrugged. 'The thing is, Kitty tries to pair me off with any and every woman who strays across her path. It must be her age. Menopausal hormones out of control or something.'

The attempt at humour was met with a steely face. 'Let me endeavour to make one thing perfectly clear, Mr Wright. I wouldn't have you if you were the last man in the world and came wrapped in gold encrusted with diamonds.'

Certainly clear enough. 'The very point I was attempting to make to Kitty.' His mouth took on a rueful quirk. 'I was trying to save you any embarrassment because Kitty can be a little...persistent when she gets a bee in her bonnet. In the event I seem to have made a pig's ear of things.'

The green gaze continued to study him for a moment.

Morgan felt he understood how an insect felt when impaled on a pin. Then he saw her head go back as she strolled further into the room. 'No problem,' she said coolly. 'Just so we are absolutely clear.'

Morgan was well versed with women and he knew he was still in deep water. 'Cocktail?' he offered as Willow held out her hands to the blazing fire in the deep, ornate fireplace, her back to him. 'I always indulge when I'm at home at the weekends.'

She didn't look at him when she said, 'Thank you, a margarita would be nice.' Her voice verged on icy.

Morgan prided himself on his margaritas. After filling a mixing glass with ice and stirring with a spoon, he tipped the ice away before topping up the glass with fresh. A dash of dry vermouth and he continued stirring, aware the figure by the fire had turned to watch him. After straining the liquid he again added more ice, along with a large measure of vodka.

It was when he strained the cocktail into a frosted martini glass rimmed with salt that Willow said, 'Don't tell me. You used to be a cocktail waiter in your youth.'

His youth? He wasn't exactly at the age to push up daisies yet. Smiling, he handed her the cocktail. Her fingers touched his for a moment and a light electric current shot up his arm. 'I worked in a cocktail bar for extra money during my uni days,' he admitted easily. 'It was a good job. I enjoyed it.'

'One of those where you throw the bottles over your head and at each other?' she asked with sweet venom.

His laugh was hearty and he saw her lips twitch in response. 'The very same. At the weekends we put on quite a show.'

'Dream job for a student, I should imagine?'

'You better believe it. On lean days we'd fill up on the snacks and stuff the owner put out for the clients; he knew but he didn't mind, not while we were pulling the punters in. The tips were great too; lots of rich Americans looking for some fun and entertainment with their drinks.'

'*Lady* Americans?' she enquired too casually.

His smile deepened. 'Is that disapproval in your voice?'

'Of course not.' She tossed her head. 'Why would it be?'

He watched with interest as her blush became brilliant. Putting her out of her misery, he busied himself fixing his second Negroni as he said casually, 'Myself and the other guy in the bar were propositioned now and again as it happens. Ladies looking for a holiday fling with no strings attached, mainly.'

He turned and saw the look on her face before she could hide it. His voice amused, he drawled, 'You're shocked.'

This time she didn't deny it. After taking a sip of her drink, she said, 'It's your life.'

He decided not to tell her he'd got a steady girlfriend at the time and had left the women to his friend who'd worked with him. This idea she'd got of him being an English gigolo was too entertaining. 'And it's been a rich one to date,' he said, deadpan.

This time she almost gulped at her cocktail.

It was mean perhaps, but he found he got a buzz from teasing her, probably because he'd felt off kilter since the first time he'd set eyes on his red-haired neighbour. Ridiculous, but Willow Landon bothered him deep inside, in a small private place no one ever reached. It was irritating and inconvenient, he told himself, but it would pass. Everything did.

'So you've been here ten years?' Her voice sounded a little desperate as she made an obvious attempt to change the subject. 'You're not bored yet? No plans to leave?'

'None.' He gestured for her to be seated as he added, 'Disappointed?' just to rile her a little more.

'Why would I be concerned whether you live here or not?' she said stiffly, sitting primly on the edge of a chair.

Her skin was the colour of honey peppered with spice and the red hair was a combination of endless shades. Fighting the urge to touch her, Morgan walked to the chair furthest from Willow's and sat down, stretching out his legs and taking a swig of his Negroni. There was a short silence and as he looked at her he found he'd tired of the game. Leaning forward suddenly, he said quietly, 'We got off to a bad start, didn't we? And it hasn't improved since. Can we come to a truce? I promise I'll try not to annoy you if you try and relax a little. If nothing else it will make life easier the next time I rescue you from a burning building or whatever.'

For a moment he thought she was going to freeze him out. Then a shy smile warmed her face, her eyes. 'Do you think there's going to be a next time?' she murmured ruefully. And before he could answer, went on, 'In spite of my track record so far I promise I'm not an arsonist in the making.'

He grinned. 'I never thought you were. Unlucky maybe…'

She inclined her head. 'Thank you for that—you could in all honesty have said stupid. It must appear that way.'

His smile died, a slight frown taking its place. 'Why would I be so crass? We all make mistakes. Life is a series of learning curves. It's when we *don't* learn from them the problems start.'

She nodded, but as Morgan stared at her there was something deep and dark in the clear green eyes that disturbed him. 'You don't believe that?' he asked gently.

She finished her cocktail before she spoke and a slow heat had crept into her cheeks. '*I* believe it. It's just that…'

'Yes?' he prompted quietly, wanting to know more.

'I suppose I've found others aren't so generous. Some people expect other people to be perfect all the time.'

Some people? It had to be a man who had hurt her enough to cause that depth of pain. Telling himself to go lightly, he said softly, 'I guess you get flawed individuals in every society who are either selfish enough or damaged enough to expect perfection. Personally I'd find being with a "perfect" person hell on earth, having enough faults myself to fill a book.'

'That sort of person doesn't see their own faults though.'

Her voice had been curiously toneless. Morgan kept all emotion out of his voice when he said, 'Are you speaking from experience? And you don't have to answer that if you don't want to.'

Her eyes flickered and fell from his, but her voice was steady: 'Yes, I am.' She glanced at the clock on the mantelpiece. 'That's a beautiful clock. Unusual.'

Morgan accepted the change of conversation with good grace although he found he was aching to know more. 'It's a French timepiece I picked up at an auction in France some years ago. The clock itself is mounted in a stirrup and horseshoe. I like unusual things. Things that don't follow a pattern. Unique things.'

Her gaze moved to the two bronze figures either side of the clock, each in the form of dancing fauns. 'I can see that. Are the fauns French too? They're very beautiful.'

'Italian, eighteenth century.'

They continued discussing the various objects of art in the room in the couple of minutes before Kitty put her head round the door to say dinner was ready, but Morgan found it difficult to concentrate. Who was this man who'd hurt her so badly? If it was a man. But it had to be; he felt it in his bones. What had he been to her and how had she got mixed up with him in the first place? Not that it was any of his business, of course.

He took Willow's arm as they walked through to the dining room where Kitty had set two places. She had lit candles in the middle of the table and the lights were dimmed; clearly their discussion about her matchmaking had had no effect at all.

Willow's hair smelt of peach shampoo, which was fairly innocuous as perfume went; why it should prompt urges of such an erotic nature the walk to the dining room was a sweet agony in his loins, he didn't know. He glanced down at the sheen of her hair as he pulled out her chair for her and resisted the impulse to put his lips to it.

Pull yourself together. The warning was grim. He was acting like a young boy wet behind the ears and on his first date with a member of the opposite sex, not a thirty-five-year-old man who had shared his bed and his life with several women in his time; some for a few months, some longer. Experience told him Willow Landon was not the sort of woman who would enter into a light relationship for the hell of it, she was too…

What was she? the other section of his mind, which was working dispassionately, asked. Clingy? Trusting? Stifling?

No. None of those. The opposite in fact. She didn't

strike him as a woman who had marriage and roses-round-the-door in mind. From what he could ascertain so far the male of the species didn't feature highly in her estimation. But neither was she the kind of woman who would enjoy an affair for however long it lasted and then walk away with no tears or regrets. He didn't know how he'd come by the knowledge but he was sure of it.

'This is lovely.' Willow glanced round the dining room appreciatively. 'Do you always eat in such style?'

Morgan glanced round the room as though he were seeing it for the first time, his gaze moving over the table set with fine linen, silver and crystal. 'Always. Kitty takes her duties very seriously,' he added dryly, reaching for the bottle of red wine. He poured two glasses and handed Willow hers, raising his as he murmured, 'To chimney sweeps and the good work they do.'

She giggled.

It was the first really natural response he'd had and he had to swallow hard as his heart began to hammer in his ribcage. He drank deeply of the wine, needing its boost to his system. It was a fine red; enough complexity showing from the skilful blending to bring out the cherry and berry flavours without spoiling the soft oaky flavours of the French and American wood. He'd drunk enough cheap plonk throughout his university days to always buy the best once he could afford to do so.

Kitty bustled in with the first course, cajun-spiced salmon with honey crème fraîche. It was one of her specialities and always cooked to perfection so the flakes of flesh fell apart when pressed with a fork.

He watched Willow take her first bite and saw the green

eyes widen in appreciation. She ate delicately, like an elegant, well-mannered cat, her soft, full lips closing over the food and tasting it carefully. With a swiftness that surprised him he found himself wondering what it would be like to feel her mouth open beneath his, to bury his hands in the silken sheen of her hair and thrust his tongue into the secret recesses behind her small white teeth. To nibble and suck and tease her lips…

'This is delicious.' She glanced up and saw him looking at her and immediately her face became wary even though her smile was polite. The withdrawal was subtle but there nonetheless.

What the hell had gone on in her life? Morgan nodded, his voice easy when he said, 'She's a strange mixture, is Kitty. She and Jim only like the plainest of food, no frills or fancies, as she puts it, but her main interest in life is cooking fantastic dishes that are out of this world. Her tofu miso soup has to be tasted to be believed and likewise her baked Indian rice pudding with nuts, fruit and saffron. I do believe she and Jim are probably sitting down to steamed white fish and three veg as we speak, though. Good solid northern food that sticks to the ribs.'

'Don't they ever eat with you?' she asked in surprise.

'Not when I have guests. Another of Kitty's set-in-concrete ideas.' Deliberately keeping his voice casual, he said, 'Do you like cooking?'

Her small nose wrinkled. 'I suppose I don't mind it but I'm not the best in the world by any means. I do experiment at weekends now and again, but I rely on my trusty microwave during the week when I'm working. Ready meals mostly, I'm afraid.'

Aware he was itching to know more about her—a lot more—Morgan warned himself to go steady. 'Tell me about your job,' he drawled as though he were merely making polite conversation. 'What do you do and where do you work?'

He ate slowly as she spoke, pretending he wasn't hanging on every word. When she came to a natural pause he asked the question he'd been working round to all evening. 'So what made you buy Keeper's Cottage? It's a bit remote, isn't it?'

The barrier that went up was almost visible. 'I liked it.'

'There must have been other places you liked closer to your work, surely? Places you could have shared with friends, perhaps?'

For a moment he thought she was going to tell him to mind his own business. He couldn't have blamed her. Instead, after a long pause, she said coolly, 'I've done the sharing-with-friends thing for a while and I decided I wanted my own house now. I…I like my own company. Being independent is important to me.'

Neat hint for the future. Morgan smiled. 'There's a hell of a lot wants doing to the cottage as far as I understand.'

Willow shrugged. 'I'm in no rush. Things will happen in time.'

'And it's tiny. Charming,' he added hastily. 'But tiny.'

'It's more than big enough for one.'

He'd finished his salmon and took a long swallow of wine, blue eyes holding green when he murmured, 'What if you meet someone?'

'I meet people all the time, Morgan, and it doesn't affect my living accommodation.'

Her voice had been light, even suggesting amusement, but her fingers were gripping the stem of the wineglass so tightly her knuckles showed white. Vitally aware of her body language, he gave the required response of a lazy smile but found he wasn't ready to do the socially acceptable thing and leave well alone. 'I mean someone special,' he said softly. 'You're a very attractive young woman and most women in your position want a partner eventually, maybe even children one day. It would be a shame to work at getting the cottage exactly how you want it only to have to move to a bigger place.'

Her pupils had dilated, black showing stark against the clear green. Slowly she took a sip of wine, then said, 'For the record I've done the partner thing, OK? Husband, everything. I didn't like it and I have no intention of repeating what was a mistake now I have my freedom again.' Rising to her feet, she added, 'I just need to pay a visit to the cloakroom. I won't be long.'

He rose with her but didn't say a word because he couldn't. He felt as though someone had just punched him hard in the stomach. And the ironic thing, he acknowledged soberly, was that he had probably asked for it.

CHAPTER FIVE

WILLOW fled to the downstairs cloakroom, berating herself with each step. Stupid. She'd been absolutely stupid to reveal what she had. And to add that bit about her freedom...

She closed the door of the cloakroom behind her and stood with her hands pressed to her hot cheeks in the cool white and grey room. Staring at her face in the large oval mirror above the washbasin, she saw her cheeks were fiery.

He'd think she'd been insinuating she was on the market again but this time for a no-strings-attached affair or something similar. Any man would. She should just have stated she had no intention of concentrating on anything other than her career for a long, long time. That would have been enough. Impersonal and to the point. Instead she'd launched into an explanation that had embarrassed them both. And Morgan *had* been embarrassed, she could tell from the look on his face. He hadn't known what to say. In fact he'd done a goldfish impression as she'd left.

Which was probably a first.

The thought came from nowhere but in spite of her agitation it made her smile for a moment. She dared bet

Morgan Wright was never taken by surprise and usually had an answer to everything.

Shutting her eyes tightly, she groaned under her breath. He really must think she was a nutcase now. First she nearly set his summerhouse on fire and covered his garden in ash, then she nearly set her own house on fire and now she was bending his ear about her disastrous marriage. What on earth was the matter with her? But he *had* asked.

Her eyes snapping open, she shook her head at herself. No excuses. He'd been making friendly dinner conversation, that was all. He hadn't asked for a precise of her lovelife to date, for goodness' sake. She hadn't been thinking clearly enough, that was the trouble. When he'd mentioned children he'd touched a nerve. She had always thought she'd be a mother one day; she'd never really imagined anything else. Perhaps she'd hung in there with Piers long after she'd known she should have left because of the dream of babies and a family? By the time she'd petitioned for divorce she'd known she'd rather be barren for the rest of her days than have Pier's child though.

Of course you didn't have to be married or with someone to have a baby these days—the world was full of single mothers who'd got pregnant knowing they had no intention of staying with the father of their child for ever. One of her city friends had been quite open about the fact she'd purposely conceived knowing she didn't even want to see the man again once she was pregnant. A high-powered businesswoman who was as ruthless in her lovelife as her worklife, Jill had already hired a full-time nanny before her baby was born and, now little Lynsey was six months old, appeared as happy as a bug in a rug with life.

But she wasn't like Jill. Sighing, she brushed her hair back from her face. And what was right for one person wasn't necessarily right for another. She wouldn't want Jill's life, which consisted of seeing Lynsey for an hour or two in the morning and even shorter time in the evening, and weekends. She knew herself well enough to realise she was an all-or-nothing kind of girl, and if she couldn't have it all—a permanent relationship, babies, roses round the door—she'd rather have nothing. Not that her life was empty; it wasn't. She had loads of good friends, a job she enjoyed and a home she'd fallen in love with the minute she'd seen it. Beth being pregnant had unsettled her, that was all. But it would be fun being an aunty and she could slake some of her maternal longing on the poor little thing in due time.

Willow continued to give herself a stern talking-to until she left the cloakroom a few minutes later, by which time she was in control of herself once more. Feeling slightly silly at the way she'd panicked and left the table, admittedly—but reason had reasserted itself and she was confident Morgan hadn't assumed she was inviting herself into his bed. She was out of practice at conversing over dinner with a member of the opposite sex, that was the trouble, she told herself ruefully as she retraced her steps. Despite offers, since Piers she hadn't dated.

When she entered the dining room Morgan was sitting where she'd left him, staring broodingly into his wineglass. For a second she studied his face, noticing the strength in the square-boned jaw, the cleanly sculpted mouth and straight nose.

His attractiveness went far beyond looks, she thought

with a sudden jolt to her equilibrium. In spite of being a very masculine male, there was nothing bullish or brutal about him. It would be easier to dismiss him from her mind if there were.

Morgan looked up, the brilliant blue eyes unreadable. 'Did I offend you just now? And please be honest, Willow.'

'What?' Completely taken aback, she stopped in her tracks before recovering and taking her seat at the table as she said, 'No, of course not. You didn't, really.'

'Upset you, then? And again, be honest.'

She stared at him. He clearly didn't believe in pushing awkward issues under the carpet. She was about to make a dismissive reply and change the subject when she saw there was real concern in the hard face. She hesitated, colour creeping up her cheeks, and then said in a rush, 'You didn't offend *or* upset me, Morgan, I promise you. It's just that—' she took a deep breath '—I don't normally wear my heart on my sleeve.'

He nodded slowly, his voice soft when he said, 'Is it still painful to talk about?'

He had refilled her wineglass while she'd been in the cloakroom and she took a long sip to gain some time. She wanted to say she didn't wish to discuss this any further so it was with something akin to surprise she heard herself say, 'I don't love him any more if that's what you mean.'

He took the wind out of her sails for the second time in as many minutes when he said quietly, 'I don't know what I mean, to be truthful. I hadn't imagined…' He shook his head at himself. 'I guess because you *look* so young I hadn't considered something like marriage. Nothing so serious or…permanent.'

Tonelessly, she said, 'I met Piers six years ago and we married eight months later. I—I was very unhappy.' She stared into the wineglass, swirling the ruby-red liquid as she spoke. 'He wasn't who I thought he was before we married. I knew I'd made a terrible mistake within the first few months but—' she shrugged '—I thought I could make it work if I tried. I was wrong. Something happened—' a few drops of wine escaped the glass, staining the linen tablecloth like blood '—and I left. We're now legally divorced. End of story.' She raised her eyes, her smile brittle. 'Just one of many said little tales happening up and down the country.'

'Perhaps. But this is *your* tale and marriage.'

'Was.' As she spoke Kitty bustled in with the main course, and Willow had never been so glad of an interruption in all her life. 'Something smells wonderful,' she said brightly.

'Steak with red-wine butter,' said Kitty cheerfully. 'You don't go in for all that slimming carry-on, do you?'

'Not me.' She had lost so much weight in the aftermath of the break-up with Piers she'd fought for months to gain weight, not lose it, having gone down to skin and bone—as Beth had put it. She'd never been voluptuous but she liked her curves.

'Good. Can't abide lettuce eaters. There's toffee-ripple cheesecake with fudge sauce for dessert. It's quite rich so you won't manage much but it's one of Morgan's favourites.'

'All your desserts are my favourites, Kitty.'

Kitty gave a rich chuckle. 'Go on with you.' But she was red with pleasure as she left them.

Willow looked at him. She was beginning to realise Morgan was more complex than she'd initially thought.

She'd felt comfortable putting him down as a wealthy bachelor with a different girlfriend for each day of the week and a jumbo ego the size of a small mountain. The first part was probably still true, but he didn't act like a man who had an inflated opinion of himself. He was obviously intelligent and determined—no one got to where he had without possessing such qualities along with a healthy dose of tenacity and intuitiveness—but he wasn't brash or conceited. And the way he was with Kitty was lovely.

She frowned to herself. She would have preferred he stayed in the box she'd put him in; it was far more comfortable. Determined to deflect more searching questions, as the door closed behind Kitty she said, 'Well, now you know all about me, how about you? Ever been tempted to walk up the aisle or are you much too sensible for that? You strike me as the confirmed-bachelor sort.'

Morgan smiled as she'd meant him to. 'I got my fingers burnt a long time ago when I was knee-high to a grasshopper,' he said lightly. 'I decided then I wasn't a for-ever-after type.'

'Then we're two of a kind.' That sounded too cosy and, feeling flustered, she took a big bite of her steak. It was wonderful. 'I'm surprised you aren't as big as a house if you eat like this all the time,' she said, raising her head.

The piercing blue eyes were waiting for her. 'Ah, but I'm only here weekends,' he pointed out softly. 'Weekdays I live in London in a very modern, functional apartment, the kitchen of which, I must confess, is rarely used.'

'You eat out all the time?'

'I work out at the gym most nights and they have a good

restaurant, which prides itself on the healthy options. I feel I can indulge at weekends. That's my excuse, anyway.'

'That doesn't sound as though you leave much time for a social life.' The words had popped out before she realised how nosy she sounded. She just hoped he didn't think she was prying.

There was a sexy quirk to Morgan's mouth when he murmured, 'Oh, I manage fairly well. On the whole.'

She just bet he did. Her gaze fell to his hand as he drank from his wineglass. His hands were like the rest of him, powerfully masculine, and his forearms were muscular and dusted with dark hair. The room was large and impressive and yet he dominated it with his presence. She could imagine he would be devastating to come up against in the business world. Devastating altogether. Not a man you could easily forget.

Even more flustered, she concentrated on her meal for the next little while, which wasn't hard because every mouthful was heavenly. Morgan did the same, eating with obvious enjoyment and making amusing small talk, which needed very little response on her part. Nevertheless she was aware she was as taut as piano wire and conscious of every little movement from the hard male body opposite her, even when she wasn't looking at him. He was an…unsettling man, she decided as Kitty cleared away their empty plates and brought two helpings of toffee-ripple cheesecake, Morgan's being large enough for half a dozen people.

He saw her glance at his plate and smiled the crooked grin that was becoming familiar to her. 'Kitty thinks I'm a growing boy. And I don't want to disillusion her, now, do I?'

It was somehow disturbingly endearing, and to combat

the quiver of something she didn't want to put a name to Willow's voice was deliberately dry when she said, 'Be careful you don't grow too much. Those extra pounds creep up on you, you know.'

'Not me. Fast metabolism.'

'All in the genes?' she asked, just to make conversation and echoing what he'd said to her earlier.

'Probably.' His voice was pleasant but dismissive.

'Your father's or your mother's?'

He stared at her for a moment and Willow saw what she could only describe as a shutter come down over the brilliant blue of his eyes in the second before he shrugged. 'Your guess is as good as mine. They died when I was too young to remember them.'

Quickly, she said, 'I'm sorry. Mine died a few months before I got married but I still miss them dreadfully. So does my sister. She's expecting a baby soon and it would have been nice for Mum to be around to see her first grandchild.' She was gabbling but the look in his eyes had thrown her. 'Do you have any brothers or sisters?' she added weakly.

He shook his head. 'No, there's just me. The one and only original. Like that clock you liked so much.'

Willow smiled because she knew he wanted her to and for the same reason didn't pursue what was clearly a no-go area. Her tenseness had given her the beginning of a headache, but she felt every moment in Morgan's company was electric so perhaps it wasn't surprising. She didn't think she had ever met anyone who was such an enigma.

They took coffee in the drawing room where Kitty had placed the tray on a low coffee table pulled close to the fire, a box of chocolates and another of after-dinner mints next to the white porcelain cups. When Morgan sat down on a two-seater sofa in front of the table Willow felt she had no option but to join him, anything else would have appeared churlish, but she took care no part of her body touched his.

She declined cream or sugar in her coffee; the cocktails had been potent and so had the wine and suddenly she felt she needed all her wits about her. The coffee was strong but not bitter and the chocolate she chose was sweet and nutty. The red glow from the fire, the mellow light in the room, the different tastes on her tongue and not least the dark man sitting quietly beside her created a whole host of emotions she could have done without. She felt tinglingly, excitingly alive and had to force her hand not to shake when she replaced her cup on the saucer and turned to Morgan. 'Thank you for dinner and everything you've done,' she said steadily. 'I'll try and be out of your hair as soon as possible tomorrow.'

'No need.' His voice was deep, smoky. She had to clench her stomach muscles against what it did to her. 'Stay as long as you like. I wasn't doing anything special this weekend.'

'Nevertheless I'd like to make a start on clearing up as soon as I can,' she prevaricated quickly. 'Get it over with.'

'I'll help you,' he offered softly.

'No, that's all right, you've done enough already.'

'Two pairs of hands will make lighter work.'

'No, really.' She could hear the tightness in her voice herself. Swallowing hard, she forced a smile. 'But thank you.'

'Is it me or are you like this with all men?'

His voice had been calm, unemotional, but the effect of his words brought her pent-up breath escaping in a tiny swoosh. Feigning a hauteur she didn't feel, she said, 'I'm sorry?'

He had settled himself in a corner of the sofa half-turned towards her and with one arm stretched along the top of the seat. The casual pose emphasised her own tenseness, which was unfortunate. 'You're as jumpy as a kitten around me,' he murmured. 'A little Titian-haired kitten with enormous green eyes that doesn't know whether to bite or purr.'

Willow bristled immediately, the welcome flood of adrenalin sharpening her voice as she said, 'I can assure you I have no intention of doing either and I am most certainly not "jumpy", as you put it. I'd just prefer to tackle my house myself, that's all.'

'So you're not frightened of me or nervous in any way?'

'Of course I'm not. Don't be so ridiculous,' she said firmly.

'That's good.'

He shifted position slightly and her bravado faltered before she steeled herself to remain perfectly still. He was only reaching for his coffee, for goodness' sake! What was the matter with her? She had to pull herself together and fast.

Morgan drank deeply from his cup, took a couple of chocolates and then settled back into the contours of the sofa, his eyes on her wary face. 'So,' he drawled lazily, 'Keeper's Cottage is the place where you hide away from the big, bad world?'

He had hit the nail square on the head but Willow would rather have walked stark naked through the village than admit it. 'Not at all.' She found she was glaring at him and quickly moderated her expression. 'I simply liked the area, the cottage, and it was the right price. It all came together at the right time.'

'I see.' His tone reeked of disbelief.

'I'm not hiding away like a hermit after my divorce, if

that's what you're suggesting,' she said hotly. 'Not for a minute.'

'That's good,' he said again.

'But even if I was—which I'm not—it would be my own business and no one else's. *No one else's.*'

'Of course it would,' he said soothingly.

Willow drew in a deep breath. 'Has anyone ever told you you're the most aggravating man in the world?' she said stonily.

Amused blue eyes considered her discomfiture. 'Not that I can remember. There have been other accolades, though.'

Willow took refuge in dignified silence—only because she silently acknowledged she wouldn't win in a war of words with Morgan. After another two chocolates she ran out of something for her hands and mouth to do. His eyes were waiting for her when she nerved herself to glance his way.

'This might not be the best time to confess, but I've arranged for a team of professional cleaners to go into the cottage first thing tomorrow,' he said coolly. 'I hope that's OK?'

'What?' She literally couldn't believe her ears.

Her voice had been so shrill he winced when he said, 'Come on, they'll do in a few hours what would take you a few days.'

'You've hired *strangers* to go into my home? How *dare* you?'

'They're not strangers, they're a small family firm I've used professionally several times and they're totally trustworthy.'

'They're strangers to *me*,' she ground out furiously.

He gave her a hard look. 'So you'd rather struggle for days and still not do such a good job as they'll accomplish.'

'Absolutely.' She glared at him.

He folded his arms over his chest, stretching his long legs as he studied her with an air of exasperation. 'You like to make it almost impossible for anyone to help you, obviously.'

'I don't want strangers in my home,' she repeated stubbornly. 'I'm sorry but you'll have to cancel them.'

'You mean it, don't you?' His voice carried a faint air of bewilderment, which would have made her smile in different circumstances. 'You'd really rather do it yourself.'

Willow tilted her chin. 'I know you were trying to be kind,' she said steadily. 'I appreciate that, really. But I am more than capable of looking after myself and I like to do things my way. I do not want a cleaning team in my cottage.'

Morgan said nothing for a few moments. Then he nodded slowly. 'Fair enough. I'll ring them and tell them they're not needed. OK?'

'Thank you.' She relaxed a little. Bad mistake.

'And in the morning I'll help you make a start and you can tell me exactly how you want things done.' He reached for another chocolate as he spoke, popping it into his mouth before offering her the box. 'OK?' he said mildly. And he smiled.

She stared at him. After rejecting his proposal about the cleaners she didn't feel she could refuse his help again. Besides, he was talking about it as though it were already a fait accompli. Her brow slightly furrowed, she said hesitantly, 'I don't want to put you about any further.'

'You're not.' He grinned a slightly wolfish grin. 'Have one of the dark ones with the cherry on top. They're delicious.'

CHAPTER SIX

OK, so he'd lied about the cleaners but it was only a small white lie. And perfectly acceptable in the circumstances.

After an hour or two of tossing and turning Morgan had given up all hope of sleep and decided to take a shower. Now, as he stood under the cool water with his face up-turned to the flow, he found his mind was still centred on the flame-haired, green-eyed girl sleeping under his roof.

She would never have agreed to let him accompany her to the cottage tomorrow without a spot of subterfuge, and the job of cleaning up was too much for one, he told himself self-righteously. Hell, he was doing her a favour after all. He'd brought home a briefcase full of papers needing his attention this weekend; it wasn't as if he didn't have anything better to do.

Turning off the water, he raked back his hair and stepped out of the shower. The bathroom was black and white, the white bath, basin, toilet and bidet offset by gleaming black wall and floor tiles and a large strip of mirror that coiled round the room at chest height and reached the ceiling. The room had a voyeuristic quality, which Morgan didn't apologise for in the least, having designed it himself, along with the equally luxurious and dramatic bedroom, again in black and white.

After drying himself roughly with a towel he walked through to the bedroom stark naked, flinging himself on the ruffled black sheets and switching on the massive high-definition LCD TV. He flicked through umpteen channels before throwing down the remote with a grunt of irritation, his mind replaying the last few minutes before he'd left Willow at her bedroom door.

He'd wanted to kiss her so why the devil hadn't he? he asked himself testily. Just a light, friendly kiss, nothing heavy. A social exchange that would have emphasised he was merely being neighbourly in having her stay. But he hadn't wanted her to get the wrong idea, to imagine he was coming on to her. She was already like a cat on a hot tin roof most of the time—he hadn't liked the idea of unsettling her further.

Nice rationalisations, another section of his mind stated dryly, but that was all they were. The truth was he hadn't dared trust himself to kiss her. He had the feeling once his mouth connected with hers it might mean a whole lot of trouble.

Groaning softly, he rolled over and stood up, pulling on his black towelling robe. If he wasn't going to be able to sleep he might as well make himself a pot of coffee and do some work in the study. He'd brought home the details of a merger he was contemplating and he wanted to get the facts and figures securely under his belt for a meeting on Monday morning. His main business interests revolved around the buying and selling of companies—always at a profit—and he had a team of people working for him at the premises he owned in the city. This project was a little different, however. A friend he'd been at uni with had approached him asking for his help. His friend owned a glass-making business, which had been handed down through his family for generations, but it was in severe financial trouble. The proposal was that for a share of the business he plough in the necessary funds to keep it floating but, friend or not, he didn't intend to try to patch up a ship that was too full of leaks. He needed to go through the papers very carefully so he knew exactly what was entailed.

The dogs were sprawled in the hall when he padded downstairs, his bare feet making no sound. Bella raised her head, wagged her tail and settled down to sleep again and the rest of the pack—as always—followed her lead. As he approached the kitchen he saw a dim light shining from under the door and, forewarned, opened the door quietly. She was sitting on one of the stools at the island in the center of the room sipping at a mug of something or other. The sight of her—her slim figure wrapped in a white towelling robe and her shining mass of hair loose about her shoulders—took his breath away for a moment. 'Willow?' he murmured softly. 'Is everything all right?'

The jump she gave almost sent her off the stool and onto the floor as she swung round to face him. 'Morgan, I didn't hear you.'

'Sorry.' He raised his hand placatingly. 'I didn't mean to startle you. I was just going to get myself some coffee.'

'No, no, that's OK, you didn't startle me.'

He clearly had. She still looked scared to death.

'I—I couldn't sleep,' she stammered. 'Strange bed. I thought I'd make myself some hot milk.'

Hot milk. He could give her something much more satisfying than hot milk to help her sleep. There was nothing like a long bout of lovemaking to relax tense muscles. 'I couldn't sleep either but in my case it's not the bed,' he said blandly. 'My solution was going to be coffee and work.' He waved his hand vaguely in the direction of his study.

She was as flushed as if she'd read his illicit thoughts, her eyes dropping to the mug in her hand. She had small hands, he thought, although her fingers were long and slender. Nice nails. Long but not too long. How would it feel to have them rake his back gently in the moment he brought her to a climax? To have her moan and pulse beneath him? To cry out as he tasted and pleased her until her thighs shook and she sobbed his name in utter abandonment? They would be good together; he knew it.

His erection pulsed, almost painfully so, and conscious the towelling robe did little to hide his arousal he kept his back to her while he fixed himself a pot of coffee, making small talk as he did so. Hell, what a situation to be in. In spite of himself he wanted to smile. If anyone had told him a few weeks ago he'd be lusting after a woman to the point of making a damn fool of himself—a woman who wasn't remotely interested in him, incidentally—he'd have told them they were crazy.

Once his body was under his control again, he reached for a cake tin and opened it to reveal one of Kitty's unsurpassable moist fruit cakes. 'Fancy a slice?' he asked as he turned and showed Willow the cake. 'It's second to none. I can guarantee you won't taste fruit cake like this again.'

'You've convinced me.'

She smiled such a friendly smile it made him feel a swine for his lecherous thoughts.

He cut them both a generous portion and joined her on the other stool. After her first bite, she said, 'It *is* fabulous. I thought my mother had the record for fruit cake but Kitty would have given her a run for her money.'

'What happened with your parents?' he asked softly. 'Was it an accident?'

She nodded, her silky hair fanning her cheeks. Quietly and softly she told him the details and, although her voice was matter-of-fact, the pain in her eyes told its own story. He didn't like how it affected him. He didn't like how *she* affected him, but he reminded himself it didn't really matter in the scheme of things. The circumstances that had thrown them together this weekend were unlikely to be repeated, and as long as he kept his lurid thoughts—and his hands—to himself, there was no harm done. Apart from a few sleepless nights perhaps.

Aiming to bring the conversation and her thoughts to happier things, he said quietly, 'You said your sister is expecting a baby soon. How does it feel knowing you'll be an aunty? Are you looking forward to it?'

She smiled, wiping a crumb from the fruit cake from the corner of her lips, and as his gaze followed the action his traitorous body responded sharply, causing his breath to catch in his throat.

'I can't wait,' she said with genuine warmth, 'but at the same time it doesn't feel quite real. I mean, Beth's my sister, the person I argued and fought and shared secrets with over the years. Her stomach's getting bigger and she's developed an obsession for chocolate and cherry muffins, but it's hard to believe there's a little person in there. Does that sound silly?'

Secretly enchanted she had let her guard down for once, Morgan shook his head. 'Not at all. I'm a mere man, don't forget. I find the whole process baffling. Well, apart from the beginning, of course. I worked out the birds and the bees some time ago.'

She giggled, blushing slightly, and as he looked at her parted lips he wanted to kiss her so hard it hurt. As he raised his eyes to hers they were smiling into his and for several seconds, seconds that quivered with intimacy, their gaze held. When her eyes dropped to her plate and she ate a morsel of cake with uncharacteristic clumsiness, dropping half of it onto the worktop, he knew he had been right.

Willow Landon was no more indifferent to him than he was to her. Which presented a whole load of new problems. Big ones.

By the time Willow returned to her room all the good work the soothing hot milk had wrought was completely undone. Morgan had escorted her to the door, said goodnight very politely and disappeared along the landing to his own room without a backward glance, thereby rendering all her fears null and void.

Fears? a little voice in the back of her mind queried nastily. Don't you mean hopes? Desires? Longings?

Her jaw tightened and she leaned back against the bedroom door, her legs trembling as she fought for control.

She was *not* attracted to Morgan Wright. 'I'm not,' she reiterated weakly, as though someone had argued the point. 'No way, no how.' She had no intention of getting involved with a man for a long, long time—if ever—and certainly not one like Morgan. If and when someone came along she could see herself dating now and again, he'd have to be a mild, retiring type who was easy-going and happy to meet her halfway on any issues that might crop up. Morgan didn't meet the criteria in any direction.

Not that he'd asked her for a date, of course. And wouldn't. It didn't need the brain of Britain to work out the sort of female Morgan would take to bed when the need arose. Without a doubt they'd be stunningly beautiful and sexy and probably highly intelligent as well; he didn't strike her as a man who would be satisfied with merely an accommodating body. He'd expect mental as well as physical stimulation from his partners.

Levering herself away from the door, she walked across to the bed and sank down. She had known all along it was madness to come into his home. One of the reasons she had bought the cottage was because of its secluded location. It was far enough away from the nearby village to ensure there'd be no pressure from neighbours intent on including her in this, that and the other, or—which was even more pertinent—if any tried, she could cold-shoulder them without having to bump into them each day.

She raised her head and glanced around the luxurious room, her conscience kicking in as it usually did.

She was grateful to Morgan for his help, she really was, and she didn't want to hurt his feelings or anyone else's for that matter, but it was somehow essential that her life was her own again down to the smallest decision. She had done the whole trying-to-please-everyone thing to death. She was never going to relinquish the tiniest fragment of her autonomy again.

Wasn't that verging on callous? questioned Soft-hearted Willow reprovingly. Wasn't that selfish and mean?

No. It was sheer self-survival, answered Unmovable, Resolute Willow grimly. Pure and simple.

Easing out a breath, she stood up. She was going to brush her teeth and go to sleep, and if Morgan insisted on helping her clean the cottage in the morning she'd thank him sincerely when they'd finished and then that would be the end of this… She sought for a word to describe what she was feeling and then gave up. 'Whatever,' she muttered grumpily to herself as she marched into the en-suite to brush her teeth.

Willow awoke to bright autumn sunshine streaming in the window the next morning. Sleepily she told herself she should have closed the curtains the night before, but then she checked the time by her wristwatch and shot into a sitting position. *Ten o'clock?* It couldn't be that late, surely? Pushing her hair out of her eyes, she refocused her gaze. Ten o'clock it was.

Springing out of bed, she galloped into the bathroom for a quick wash and brush-up and was dressed and ready to venture downstairs within five minutes, her hair pulled back in a high ponytail and her face clean and scrubbed. She couldn't believe she'd slept so late. When he had left her the night before Morgan had mentioned he normally breakfasted about eight in the morning at the weekends. What must he be thinking? And Kitty—the housekeeper would obviously have expected her employer's guest to eat with him. Yet again she had done the wrong thing.

The big house was quiet and still when Willow opened

her bedroom door and stepped onto a galleried landing flooded with light. Old houses were sometimes dark and somewhat forbidding, but due to the number of large windows on every floor of this one it breathed airiness and space. She stood for a moment breathing in the slightly perfumed air, the source of the delicate scent becoming apparent when she descended the stairs and saw a huge bowl of white and yellow roses on a table at the foot of the staircase. They had obviously been arranged by Kitty earlier.

She didn't have time to think about the flowers, though. As Willow reached the bottom step Morgan uncurled himself from one of the easy chairs dotted about the vast hall, throwing down the magazine he'd been reading before her arrival.

'I'm so sorry,' she said before he could speak. 'I never sleep late, never, and you told me what time breakfast was. I hope I haven't put Kitty out and—'

'Easy, easy.' He smiled with warm amusement in his eyes. 'In this house the weekends fit in with the occupants, not the other way round. You clearly found the bed comfortable at least.'

In truth she had tossed and turned until dawn, but her inability to sleep had had nothing to do with the bed and all to do with the tall dark man in front of her. 'It was lovely, thank you.' She could hear the breathlessness in her voice and was annoyed by it. The night before she had decided she was going to be very calm, cool and collected in her future dealings with Morgan Wright and here she was acting like a gauche fourteen-year-old.

'Jim's taken Kitty shopping once I persuaded her we were quite capable of sorting ourselves out for breakfast,' he said lazily. 'I suggest we eat in the kitchen if that's OK? It's easier and Kitty's not here to object.'

'That's fine by me but you should have eaten earlier.' She felt awful having clearly put a spanner in the house's normal weekend routine. It was so rude.

'Why would I do that?' he said quietly, walking her through to the kitchen at the end of the hall.

Morgan opened the door and stood aside for Willow to precede him into the room. The kitchen was fabulous. She'd seen it in dim light, last night, but she'd been too fraught to take in how stunning it was. The flowing lines of the spectacularly beautiful black granite worktops, which glittered like a starry night's sky, the wide expanse of light wood cupboards and array of every modern appliance known to man were impressive. 'Wow,' she breathed. 'Now this *is* a kitchen.'

'Like it?' He smiled, obviously pleased. 'This is Kitty's domain but I designed it myself and know my way around.' He walked to a refrigerator that could have accommodated several families, opening it as he said, 'There's orange, grapefruit, apple and mango, black grape and cranberry juice. Which would you like? Oh, and a couple of smoothies, banana and loganberry.'

'No pineapple?' she asked, tongue in cheek.

He looked at her and she looked at him. He stood enveloped in the golden sunlight streaming through the wide kitchen window, his black jeans and white shirt making him a living monochrome. Her heart stopped and then galloped as he smiled slowly, his blue eyes warm as he said, 'Touché.'

'I'll have black grape, please,' she said weakly after a long moment when she could find her breath to speak.

He wasn't supposed to be able to laugh at himself. Her heart was now thumping like a gong in her chest and she wasn't able to control her breathing. That wasn't who Morgan Wright was. *Was it?* But then she didn't have a clue who he was.

She sat down at the kitchen table, which had been set for two. Not by Kitty, she was sure. A basket of what looked like home-made soft rolls and a pat of butter were in the centre, and Willow suddenly felt ravenously hungry. As Morgan handed her a glass of juice she said, 'May I?' as she nodded at the rolls.

'Help yourself.' He grinned. 'Cooked this morning by Kitty's fair hand. No shop-bought bread in this establishment.'

'You're spoilt,' she said a moment later, her mouth full of the delicious bread. 'Absolutely spoilt rotten.'

'You're right.' He'd begun to cook bacon and eggs and the aroma was heavenly. 'And long may it continue.'

They ate sitting side by side in the sunlit kitchen, finishing off with some of the best coffee Willow had ever tasted. Replete, she stretched like a slender well-fed cat. 'I've never eaten three eggs at one sitting in my life.' She glanced at him and he was smiling. 'It's not good for you, you know,' she said reprovingly. 'Very bad for your health, in fact.'

'Eating?' he murmured mockingly.

'Eating too many eggs.'

'You've been listening to the experts, I take it?' he drawled lazily. 'Give it another decade and they'll be saying you should eat a dozen a day or something. Their advice changes with the wind. There's always someone saying something different.'

'So how do you know what's right?'

He gave her a long, steady look and suddenly they weren't talking about eggs. His eyes held hers locked. 'Go with your heart,' he said softly. 'Always with your heart.'

There was a silence that stretched and lengthened. 'And if your heart lets you down and leads you astray?' she said shakily. 'What happens then?'

'There's no guarantees in life,' Morgan acknowledged after a moment, 'but what's the alternative? To live in fear and never experience the freedom of casting all restraint aside?'

'Eggs aren't that important to me in the overall scheme of things,' she said with forced lightness. 'I could live without them.'

'Pity.' He studied her face. 'What if you wake up one day years from now when it's too late and you're old and set in your ways and regret all those breakfasts you never had? What then?'

'At least my cholesterol will be under control.'

'And control is important to you?' he asked smoothly.

Again he'd put his finger on the nub of the issue but this time she wasn't going to let him get away with it. Remembering their conversation of the day before, she said carefully, 'Probably as important as it is to you, yes.'

His mouth quirked to the side, a self-deprecating smile that intensified his attractiveness tenfold. 'Ouch,' he murmured lazily. 'I guess I set myself up for that one.'

Willow slid off her chair. 'I'll help you clear up so all's as it should be when Kitty comes back.'

'No need, it won't take a minute to load the dishwasher. Why don't you get your bag and meet me in the hall and we'll go to the cottage and start?' he said easily.

Willow hesitated. She knew she didn't want Morgan in her cottage. It was too—her mind balked at dangerous and substituted—irksome. But she also knew he'd made up his mind he was going to help.

Her expression must have spoken for itself because he said, very softly, 'Get your bag, Willow.'

They worked like Trojans the rest of the day until late in the evening. Kitty arrived with lunch about one o'clock but apart from that they didn't take a break. Willow had to admit Morgan did the work of ten men and by seven o'clock the cottage was cleaner than it had ever been. Morgan had thought to bring a large container of upholstery shampoo with him and her sofa and armchair were now damp but free of smuts. The new sitting-room curtains she'd bought the week before had been washed, dried in the sunshine and ironed and were now back in place at the squeaky-clean window. Ceiling, walls, floorboards and fireplace had been washed down and Morgan had even given the kitchen a once-over, although soot hadn't penetrated too far within its walls. The bathroom door had been shut so that room hadn't needed any attention.

Kitty had insisted she was cooking an evening meal for them when she'd brought lunch, and Willow had to admit she wasn't sorry as she took a quick shower and washed her hair, vitally conscious of Morgan sitting on the French window steps nursing a cup of coffee. She was exhausted, the result of working flat out all day and not having slept properly the night before. Not to mention the nervous tension with being around him.

She left the bathroom cocooned from head to foot in

towels and scurried up the stairs to her bedroom, even though there was no need to panic. Morgan wasn't the type of man to take advantage. He wouldn't have to, she thought wryly as she hastily got dressed in cream linen trousers and a jade-green cashmere top, which had cost an arm and a leg a few months ago. Morgan would have women falling over themselves to get noticed by him.

After drying her hair into a sleek curtain, she left it loose and applied the minimum of make-up, along with silver hoops in her ears. She wanted to look fresh and attractive but not as if she was trying too hard. After dabbing a few drops of her favourite perfume on her wrists she was ready. Taking a deep breath, she checked herself in the mirror. Wide green eyes stared anxiously back at her and she clicked her tongue irritably. For goodness' sake! She looked like a scared rabbit!

Smoothing her face of all expression, she tried a light smile. That was better. She was going to have dinner with him, that was all, and once tonight was over it was doubtful they'd run into each other again. In fact she'd make sure they didn't. Morgan was only in residence at weekends and she could avoid being home until late for the next little while. The planning office was crying out for a few folk to work Saturdays on a new project in Redditch, and on Sundays she could catch up with friends and visit Beth. It would all work out just fine.

Not that she expected Morgan to try and see her. Why would he? He was way out of her league in every way. But she didn't want him to think she was hanging around at weekends in the hope of bumping into him. That would be the ultimate humiliation.

Neurotic. The word vibrated in her head from some deep recess in her psyche and she pulled a face at the girl in the mirror before turning away defiantly. She wasn't neurotic, she argued silently, but even if she was she'd prefer that than Morgan Wright thinking she was interested in him.

Morgan was still sitting on the steps when she walked into the sitting room, his head resting on the side of one of the open French doors and his eyes shut. He hadn't had the advantage of a shower and the shirt that had been white that morning was white no longer. She had approached noiselessly and now she stood for a moment looking at him. The hair, which was longer than average for a man—or certainly a businessman—had flicked up slightly on his collar and he had smudges of dirt on his face. Beneath the shirt hard muscles showed across his chest and shoulders and his forearms were sinewy beneath their coating of soft black hair. He looked more like someone who spent his days working outside than anything else. Tough, strong, brawny. Even slightly rough and hard-bitten. Piers had been tall but slender and even beautiful in a classical Adonis sort of way.

Shocked by the knowledge that she was comparing the two of them, she must have made a noise because the next moment the brilliant blue eyes had opened. 'What's the matter?' He was instantly on the alert, rising to his feet with an animal grace that belied her earlier thoughts. 'What's happened?'

'Nothing.' She forced a smile. 'Nothing at all.'

'Nothing? Willow, you were staring at me as though I was the devil incarnate.'

'Of course I wasn't.' Somehow she managed to keep any shakiness out of her voice and smile. 'You imagined it.'

His expression hardened. 'Tell me,' he said flatly.

'There's nothing to tell. I…I was thinking your office staff might have a job to recognise their immaculately turned out boss tonight, that's all.' It was weak but all she could think of.

'I don't believe you.' His blue eyes searched her face, demanding the truth. 'What have I done to make you look like that? Forgive me, but I think I've a right to know.'

'Nothing. Really, you haven't, you know you haven't. You—you've been very kind.' He wasn't buying it. 'Very kind.'

'So tell me,' he said again. 'What were you thinking?'

Willow stared at him helplessly. 'I was thinking of my ex-husband,' she admitted flatly, knowing he wouldn't like it.

Morgan's eyes narrowed to blue slits. 'From the little you've said about him it's no compliment you look at me and see him. Are we similar to look at? Is that it?'

'No, that's not it. At least, what I mean is, you don't remind me of him. Just the opposite, in fact.'

She could tell he was unconvinced even before he folded his arms and said stiffly, 'So what brought him to mind?'

Inwardly groaning, she sought for the right words. 'Piers was very handsome,' she said slowly. 'And charming.'

He stared at her. 'Willow, this isn't getting any better.'

'What I mean is, it was all false. A front. The real Piers—' She shook her head, shuddering in spite of herself.

Willow wasn't aware of him moving and taking her into his arms, it happened so quickly, but amazingly she didn't fight the embrace but sank into it, closing her eyes as she rested against his chest. She felt his mouth on the top of her head in the lightest of kisses before he murmured, 'Don't look like that. He can't hurt you any more, it's over. He has no hold on you now, Willow.'

'I know.' She *did* know, but occasionally the memory of that last terrible night in their apartment would take over despite all her efforts to keep it at bay. Maybe Beth was right. Perhaps she should have seen a counsellor and talked things through with someone trained to help in such cases, but she had been determined to rise above the tag of victim. She still was. And as Morgan had just said, it was over now. He couldn't hurt her any more.

Making a desperate effort to pull herself together and both shocked and mortified at how the evening had degenerated into something much too raw, she moved out of Morgan's arms as she said, 'You're not like him in any way, that's what I was thinking. I promise. Not in looks or anything else.'

'Good.' Gently he pulled her close again. His kiss was thorough but gentle, the sort of kiss she had fantasised about as a young schoolgirl. She was overwhelmed with a drowning, floating sensation that was sweet and sensual at the same time and mind-blowingly addictive. She felt a soft warmth blooming deep within her body and parted her lips to strengthen the intimacy between them, not really aware of what she was doing and led purely by an instinct so strong it was overpowering.

She was pressed against the muscular wall of his chest and could feel his heart thudding his arousal. It was exhilarating, heady, to know he wanted her. In these moments of time it was all that mattered. And she wanted him too.

His fingers had tangled in her hair, tilting her head back as his lips moved over hers with more urgency, his mouth meltingly sexy. He'd moulded her into him as he'd deepened the kiss and she felt as though they were already making love standing up, every contour of his hard male body pressing against her softness. It should have shocked her but it didn't.

'Willow…' He groaned her name and something in his voice echoed in her. She wanted him. Right here and now, on the floor of her sitting room, she wanted him.

It was like a deluge of icy cold water as her mind registered how much she'd lost control. She jerked away, stumbling backwards as she gasped for air. 'No.' The word sounded plaintive, weak, and she took another breath before she said more strongly, 'I don't want this. I'm sorry but I don't want this. This is not who I am.'

Morgan was quite still. For a moment something continued to blaze in the blue eyes and then it was veiled. His control was almost insulting when he nodded, a faint smile touching his lips as he murmured, 'No problem, put it down to one of those crazy moments, OK?' As she continued to stare at him he added softly, 'I'm not a wolf, Willow. You're quite safe. No is no in my book.'

A single beat passed. She knew she had to say something. They both were aware she had been there with him every moment. Flicking her hair from her hot face, she found she couldn't look at him when she said, 'I—I didn't mean to make you think—'

'I didn't.' His voice was firm but not annoyed. 'It's fine.'

Willow swallowed hard. 'What I mean is—'

'Stop it, OK? Like I said, it was one of those crazy

moments that happen sometimes between members of the opposite sex. Now, I don't know about you but I could eat a horse so how about we see what Kitty's rustled up this evening?'

She met his eyes then. His features were expressionless and she couldn't tell what he was thinking. It was easier to take his words at face value, besides which she didn't know how to explain to him what she couldn't explain to herself. If someone had told her that morning she would want Morgan Wright to take her with every fibre of her being she would have laughed in their face, but she had. And in this moment of absolute honesty with herself she knew this had been brewing from the first time she'd laid eyes on him, but she hadn't wanted to acknowledge the fierce attraction this man held for her.

Feeling the ground beneath her feet had changed to shifting sand, she knew she couldn't dodge the truth. Gathering all her courage, she said woodenly, 'I don't make a practice of giving the wrong signals, I just want you to know that. I've never slept with anyone except my ex.'

'If you're trying to tell me you aren't the sort of woman to hop in and out of bed with any man who catches your fancy, I'd already worked that out for myself.' He raked back his hair and went on in a tone laced with unmistakable sincerity, 'You're still working things through after the break-up, I can see that, so don't beat yourself up about one kiss. That's all it was, a kiss. Forget it, Willow. I already have.'

But it hadn't been, at least not for her. It had been an introduction into a realm she'd never imagined even existed. She'd loved Piers—at first, that was—but his lovemaking had never done what one kiss from Morgan had accomplished.

Her green eyes darkened but, telling herself she had to follow his lead and lighten the mood, she nodded and smiled. 'You're right,' she said as casually as she could manage.

He returned the smile. 'Of course I'm right,' he said lazily. 'It goes with the name.' Shutting the French doors, he locked them and then turned to where she was standing, leaning forward and touching her lips lightly with his before she'd realised what he was going to do. 'We're friends,' he said easily, taking her arm and leading her out of the cottage into the warm October shadows, 'so relax. You've got nothing to fear from me.'

Willow took a breath and tried to ignore what the feel of his warm flesh on hers was doing to her equilibrium. She might not have anything to fear from Morgan—although that was a mute point—but she had plenty to fear from herself where this man was concerned. She had to remember that and be on her guard. Morgan had been kind to her and she was grateful, but there was much more to him than met the eye. Much more.

CHAPTER SEVEN

WILLOW awoke in her own bed the next morning and listened to the faint echo of the bells in the village church calling the faithful to the Sunday morning service. Sunlight spilled through the window but the air was cool as she slipped out of bed and made her way downstairs to the kitchen wrapped in her thick robe. It was sparkling clean after Morgan's spring clean.

After making herself a pot of coffee she poured a cup and wandered through to the sitting room. The sofa and chair were still a little damp from Morgan's ministrations the day before and so she opened the French doors and sat on the steps, much as he'd done. The air was actually warmer in the garden than it was in the house, she thought with a stab of surprise. The solid walls of the cottage had the effect of cooling the rooms somewhat. Morgan had given her the name and telephone number of a local plumber the night before so she could see about having central heating fitted before the worst of the winter.

Morgan… She bit down on her bottom lip pensively. He'd behaved like a perfect gentleman after that one scorching kiss. They'd eaten Kitty's wonderful dinner, talked, laughed a little and enjoyed coffee with a fine liqueur before he'd seen her home to her front door. He'd tucked her hand through his arm as they had walked the short distance down his drive and into the lane before reaching the cottage, and although she'd known it was merely a casual gesture it had seemed strangely intimate to feel the pressure of his body close to hers. Once at her door she had prepared herself for the goodnight kiss. Only it hadn't come. Not even a fleeting peck like the one he'd given her after the scorcher. She could have been his maiden aunt, she thought crossly.

Willow frowned to herself, inhaling the fragrant scent of coffee as she idly watched two blue tits hanging from a nut feeder she'd hung from one of the trees bordering the garden, their distinct blue crests on tiny black and white heads vivid in the sunshine.

Not that she had *wanted* him to kiss her, she assured herself firmly. The close embrace hours before had been enough to convince her that where Morgan was concerned she'd be playing with fire. No, far better to keep it light and easy. And that was exactly what he'd done. Her frown deepened. Which was fine.

She finished the coffee and fetched another cup, settling herself down again in the same spot and feeling intensely irritable.

She was being ridiculous. She nodded to the thought. *And* hypocritical, which was the one human failing she loathed above all others. A hot arrow of guilt pierced her. She couldn't insist Morgan kept his hands—and his mouth—to himself and then feel miffed when he did exactly that. She was being monumentally unfair and capricious and unreasonable, but *why* hadn't he mentioned seeing her again? Why had he just walked off without a word?

Because you're just the neighbour he helped out.

She lifted one shoulder in answer to the thought, the motion defensive, almost aggressive. In that case he'd had no right to kiss her as he had, had he? She took a long pull at the coffee, scalding hot though it was. He hadn't; it had been grossly unfair.

She *was* being ridiculous. He'd explained that kiss as one of those things that happened now and again between members of the opposite sex, and that was what it had been. It wasn't his fault that it had been the most devastatingly, incredible, *amazing* experience of her life and had left her wanting much, much more.

Her heart jolted violently and then jump-started itself into a machine-gun gallop. She put her hands to her chest as though to calm it down, her mind racing.

No, no, no. She shut her eyes tightly as she struggled for calm. He had said friends and that was exactly what their relationship—*relationship?*—was. Friends. Neighbours. Nothing more. Nothing less. Anything more would be disastrous.

She opened her eyes. The blue tits were back, having been disturbed temporarily when she'd gone to fetch her second cup of coffee. They twittered happily, positively frolicking on the nuts.

She had no right to feel let down. No right at all, and yet she did. More than she could have imagined. Which only proved she had been absolutely right when she had told herself that Morgan Wright was dangerous and to be avoided.

* * *

'So she didn't stay another night?' Kitty said disapprovingly.

Morgan clenched his teeth but when he spoke his voice was cool and controlled. 'No, Kitty, she didn't.'

'Pity.' Kitty sucked her breath through her teeth. 'Pity.'

'Pity?' Even as he told himself not to bite, he responded.

'I think so. She seems a nice young lady.'

'Ah, but I go for the bad ones, Kitty. You should know that by now.' He grinned at her with a lecherous wink.

Kitty treated his mockery with the contempt it deserved and ignored it as she plonked Morgan's breakfast in front of him. 'So when are you seeing her again?' she said stolidly.

Morgan deliberately finished the last of his coffee before he said, 'I've no idea. When she needs rescuing from a burning building or something similar? That seems to be the pattern.'

Kitty surveyed him, hands on hips. Even her apron seemed to rustle with indignation. 'You didn't arrange to see her again? A lovely young woman like that? Why ever not?'

He had asked himself the same question countless times and the answer didn't sit well with him. Willow had the potential to complicate his autonomous controlled life and he needed that sort of aggravation like a hole in the head. In fact it scared the hell out of him. Pouring himself more coffee, he said casually, 'Why would I arrange to see her, Kitty? She's a neighbour who needed a helping hand, that's the only reason she came here in the first place.' He took a sip and burnt his mouth.

'Maybe, but she did come and you seemed to get on well.'

Get on well? He was drawn to Willow with a strength that he hadn't felt before and that was the very reason he had to avoid contact. Shrugging, he murmured, 'She was polite and grateful, but I think getting on well might be pushing it a bit. Besides which—' He stopped abruptly. Was it wise to go on?

'What?' Kitty's ears pricked up immediately.

'Nothing.' And then he decided to tell her. If nothing else it might stop her infernal matchmaking. 'She's not in the market for any sort of relationship, as it happens. She was married and I gather the divorce wasn't an amicable one. Once burnt, twice shy. She doesn't date and she intends to keep it that way.'

Kitty snorted. 'Poppycock. The lass might be a bit wary, but that's better than some of these brazen types that are around these days. That's the one thing I can't abide in a woman, brazenness.'

What she meant was the brazen types *he* dated, Morgan thought wryly, being fully aware of Kitty's opinion of his lifestyle and in particular his women. He unfolded his Sunday paper, signifying the conversation was at an end, his voice dismissive when he said coolly, 'She's a neighbour, that's all, Kitty. And I'll have a round of toast to go with the bacon and eggs, please.'

For once Kitty wasn't playing ball. Folding her arms across her plump little stomach, she said grimly, 'You let this one go and you'll regret it, m'lad. That's all I'm saying.'

For crying out loud! His tone deliberately weary, he said, 'I can't let go of what I don't have. End of story.' And he raised the newspaper in front of his face.

He didn't enjoy his breakfast and the paper was full of

rubbish. Irritable and out of sorts, he decided to take the dogs for a long walk to blow away the cobwebs and get himself back on course so he could work that afternoon.

Pulling on a leather jacket, he whistled the dogs and left the house a few minutes later. There was a pleasing nip in the air, foretelling the frosts that were sure to come later in the month. The October day was fresh and bright, shallow sparkles of sunshine warming the fields that stretched either side of the lane beyond his house. He walked in the opposite direction to Willow's cottage and the village, a host of magpies in the trees bordering the lane chattering across the autumn sky.

Shortly after leaving his property, he turned off the lane onto a footpath that led between fields recently ploughed under the stubble of the old wheat crop, the dogs gambolling ahead but taking care to stay on the footpath like the well-trained animals they were. The landscape was already turning into a glorious world of golden tints from copper to orange and Morgan stood for a moment, breathing in the sharp air and looking up into a blue sky, which until recently had been full of swallows gathering together ready to migrate and screaming their goodbyes.

Everything was fine. He nodded to the thought. Nothing had changed. His world was ticking along nicely and under his control.

He continued to tell himself this throughout the rest of the walk and by the time he returned home he was ready for his Sunday lunch. He ate a hearty portion of Kitty's Yorkshire pudding and roast beef with roast potatoes that were crisp on the outside and feathery soft on the inside, and disappeared into his study for the rest of the afternoon. By the time he re-emerged as a golden autumn twilight was falling he had the facts and figures of the papers he'd been studying clear in his head.

He met Kitty in the hall and she was carrying a tray holding steaming coffee and a plate of her delicious home-made shortbread. 'Though you might want a break,' she said fussily. 'You work too hard.'

Morgan hid a smile. This was her way of saying he was now forgiven. 'Thanks, but I'm just on my way out,' he said, and it was only in that moment he realized he'd been intending to call round and see Willow from the moment he opened his eyes that morning. 'I'll be back as and when,' he added, 'so don't worry about dinner. I'll grab a sandwich or something when I come in. Your roast was enough to keep a man going for twenty-four hours.'

He left before she could ask any awkward questions and for the same reason took the Harley. It would have been a giveaway if he'd walked. Kitty had a nose like an elephant as it was.

When he knocked on the door of Willow's cottage his heart was slamming against his ribcage with the force of a sledgehammer and his mouth felt dry. In any other situation he could have laughed at himself. This evening, though, he didn't feel like laughing.

The door opened and he hoped his nervousness, his rush of wanting, wasn't obvious to her. She stared at him wide-eyed, her delectable mouth slightly open, and he had to swallow hard before he could say, 'Just wondering how the sofa and things are drying out.' Weak, but it was the best he could do.

'They—they're still a bit damp.' She smiled warily.

He nodded. 'Are you cold?' he asked, noticing she was wearing a big baggy furry kind of top over her jeans.

'I haven't been able to light a fire.'

No, of course she hadn't. He wasn't about to look a gift horse in the mouth. He nodded again, in a I-thought-as-much kind of way. 'I know a nice warm little pub not far from here that does wonderful meals and the Harley's waiting.'

She blinked a couple of times and then, as though regaining control over her composure, she smoothed her hair in a little-girl gesture that spoke of confusion. 'Is—is this you being friends?' she said with a monosyllabic breath of laughter.

'Absolutely.' If ever there was a situation where a lie was called for, this was it. 'Scout's honour and all that.'

Their gazes met and held for a moment before hers skittered away. He didn't know whether she liked him or not, Morgan thought triumphantly, but she damn well wasn't unaffected by him and he'd take any encouragement he could get right at this moment. 'And it's also being a good neighbour,' he added, deadpan. 'Such a quality is highly thought of in this part of the country, believe me. Part of the countryman's code and unbreakable.'

She smiled and lust, pure and hot, knifed through him. Well, hot at least. White-hot, in fact.

'OK.' She lowered her head, her hair falling in a sleek curtain either side of her face. 'Come in a minute while I change. I can't go anywhere in these old things.'

Once in the cottage the chill was obvious, even through his leather jacket. He stood, hands thrust in his jeans pockets and his gaze directed at the ceiling above which she was changing. The place was an ice-box. Concern for her brought his mouth into a straight line, moments before he told himself it was none of his business. She had made it clear the day before she was in charge of her life. Furthermore, that she wouldn't appreciate any efforts to alter the status quo. He had to respect that.

She reappeared, and his voice sounded husky even to his own ears when he said, 'Ready?' She looked like all his Christmases rolled into one: gorgeous, self-possessed and as sexy as hell. And yet the demure little top she was wearing covered her to the neck and halfway down her arms, even though it clung in all the right places. A hundred women could wear it and it wouldn't stir his pulse above normal, but on Willow…

'This is very kind of you, Morgan.'

She meant well, but he found he'd had enough of the label. 'I never do anything I don't want to do, Willow.' He smiled to soften the statement as he helped her on with her jacket. 'I'm your typical selfish male. We're born that way.'

'But honest.' She was smiling back at him as she reached for her handbag. 'Well, you are at least. Aren't you?'

'I try to be.' He nodded. 'Yes, I think I am.' Then he grinned. 'Most of the time anyway.'

'Well, I guess that's not bad for the male of the species.' Her voice was light but there was something in her tone that jarred on him. Whether she was aware of it or not, he didn't know, but immediately she followed with, 'Some females too, come to think of it. Women are more inclined to tell little white lies so as not to hurt someone's feelings, I've found.'

'You mean with answers to questions like, "Does my

bum look big in this?"' he replied lazily, to put her at ease, even as he thought, What the hell did her husband do to her to make her so sceptical? She wasn't like this before him, he'd bet money on it.

'Exactly.'

Once outside he nodded at the Harley parked across the other side of the lane. 'Hope you don't mind the mode of transport, but it won't be long and this beauty will be consigned to the garage if we get the sort of floods we got last year during the winter.'

She didn't answer this directly, saying instead as they walked over to the motorbike, 'What sort of car have you got?'

'Cars, plural. An Aston Martin and a Range-Rover.' But you won't have to hold onto me in those and I wouldn't feel your body pressed against mine. His eyes glittering, he gave her the spare helmet he'd brought with him and then helped her up behind him. She smelled gorgeous, some flowery thing with undertones he couldn't put a name to but which made his body harden. 'OK? Hold on tight.' Real tight, don't be shy.

He turned briefly to smile at her before he switched on the engine and her voice sounded breathless when she said, 'I'm not used to riding on a motorbike. How far away is the pub?'

'Not too far.' Unfortunately.

In fact it was ten minutes, being in the next village, the winding lanes that twisted and curved making it far longer than the crow flew and imposing their own speed limit. The pub was a pretty little thatched affair, complete with brasses and narrow mullioned windows and solid oak furniture. Having secured comfy seats by the big open fireplace in which a blazing fire roared, Morgan fetched two halves of beer and the menus.

'Warmer?' He took a long swallow of his beer, looking at her over the rim of his glass. She looked good enough to eat.

She nodded, her gaze not holding his but dropping to the menu in her hand as she said, 'Much. And starving too.'

They were seated at a table for two, so close he could reach out and touch her if he wanted to. And he wanted to, he acknowledged silently. But he didn't. 'The pan-fried crispy pork with red-onion gravy is seriously good here,' he said conversationally. 'But the steaks are great too. Local butcher. But perhaps you'd prefer fish or a risotto?'

'The pork sounds lovely.' She tucked her hair behind her ears as she spoke, the movement not so much wary as guarded. He wondered if she ever let that guard down. Whatever, Willow Landon was one hard female to get to know, but, remembering that burning kiss and the way it had shook him up, it would be worth the trouble. Nothing worth having came easy.

Madness. The word resonated as it bounced round his head. This was madness and he knew it, so why had he asked her out tonight when this had every chance of ending badly?

He knew why. He wanted to make love to her more than he'd wanted to make love to a woman for a long, long time. There was a gnawing hunger inside him for her body, which had been with him since he'd first met her, and it was damn uncomfortable. If he took her to bed then maybe it would assuage the primal need and she'd stop featuring in his dreams every night.

That being the case, why wasn't he going all out to

weaken her defences? another part of his mind asked caustically. He'd had enough experience with women to know the right buttons to press, for crying out loud. It was all part of the mating game.

Because Willow was different.

An alarm went off in his mind, causing him to raise his head with a jerk as a waitress appeared at their table for their order. He raised one eyebrow to Willow. 'The pork?' And at her nod, said to the waitress, 'Make that two.'

'This is nice.' She glanced round the pub as she spoke, her voice warm. 'Do you come here often?'

'Usually just the odd weekend when Kitty and Jim go to visit relatives in the north-east. Kitty always leaves meals she's prepared, but it's the putting it in the oven and getting it out at the right time I fall down on. I tend to work and invariably the meal's cremated by the time I remember.'

'She's very fond of you, isn't she?' She smiled warmly.

'As am I of her and Jim. We rub along together fairly well.'

She nodded. 'They're nice people, what my father would have called salt of the earth.'

The fact that it really mattered that she liked Kitty and Jim was another warning shot across his bows, but again he chose to ignore it. Lifting one ankle to rest it across the opposite knee, he settled back in his seat. 'Tell me about your father,' he said quietly. 'Were you close to him and your mother?'

She was silent for a moment. 'Very close. Beth was too.'

He found he wanted to know more. 'What were they like? As parents, I mean.' He wanted to picture her as a little girl.

She glanced at him, a small, uncertain look. 'They were great,' she said awkwardly.

Suddenly he understood. 'It doesn't hurt to hear about other people's parents,' he lied softly. 'Tell me, if it's not too painful to talk about them,' he added quickly.

'No, Beth and I talk about them often.' She bit her lower lip, her small white teeth worrying the flesh for a moment. 'Where do you want me to start?'

His eyes had flared at the action, but he didn't betray the desire it had induced in his voice when he said, 'The beginning. You as a little girl in pigtails and white lace.'

She smiled, as he'd wanted her to, and relaxed a little. 'I so wasn't a white lace sort of child.'

'But you had pigtails? Cute little red pigtails and freckles?'

She nodded. 'Plenty of freckles.'

'Pigtails and dungarees, then, and scabby knees and ink-stained fingers. And those sandal things, jelly beans, aren't they?'

'Now you're nearer the truth.' She took a sip of her beer and began, 'Well, Mum was a stay-at-home mother and Dad had a nine-to-five job, very traditional…' She talked about her home, their family holidays, how she and her sister had smuggled home a 'pet' crab because they'd been desperate for a pet, after which their parents had bought them a hamster each…

He listened, fascinated, but consciously untensing his jaw several times as the scenes her words invoked brought the old familiar longing tightening muscles.

The subject came to a natural conclusion when the waitress brought their meals, but for a few moments the feeling he'd grown up with—that of being on the outside looking in—was strong before he slammed the lid on what he considered weakness. Being shunted around various relatives who grudgingly took him in for a few months at a time, ignored, neglected, shouted at, was a better deal than some poor kids had, and the independence that had been forced on him at an early age had got him to where he was now. Without that early training he wouldn't have made it.

He repeated the words that had become his mantra to focus his mind on the positive as he ate, and within a minute or two he was back on an even keel. He didn't *need* anyone, he'd managed on his own for over three decades and that was the way he liked it. No, he didn't *need* anyone, but wanting physically was a different matter and entirely natural. And he wanted Willow. More and more every moment he was with her. He didn't know what it was about this defensive, wary, honey-skinned woman that made him ache with want, but whatever it was, it had knocked him for six. He admitted it. In fact it was a relief to admit it.

But it brought its own set of problems. The main one of which being he was dealing with a vulnerable young woman here, not the sort of woman he usually favoured who was capable of being as ruthless as him, in bed and out of it. Whatever had gone on with this idiot of a husband of hers, it hadn't been pleasant and the scars hadn't healed. Not by a long chalk. He had to walk away from this one. At least for a while.

Morgan's eyes narrowed but otherwise his face was impassive, displaying no emotion. This ability he had of hiding his feelings was what had made him so successful in business.

The trouble was, he didn't know if he could walk

away. A pang of desire struck, low and deep. And that left him…where? Between a rock and a hard place, as Kitty would say.

'…mine, it's pretty wonderful.'

Too late he realised Willow had spoken and he hadn't caught most of it. Pulling himself together, he said, 'Sorry?'

'I said, if your pork is as good as mine, it's pretty wonderful,' she repeated quietly, clearly slightly put out he hadn't heard her the first time. Which was understandable.

Cursing himself, he said smoothly, 'It's so good I always lose concentration for the first few mouthfuls—it's the glutton in me. Shameful, I admit it.'

She smiled, but a faint shadow remained in the green eyes. He didn't like that he'd put it there, nor the uncertainty that went with it. Which was crazy, he told himself grimly. When had he ever cared to that extent? It was further proof, if any were needed, that he had been right. He had to walk away now and stop flirting with disaster. There were plenty of Charmaines out there, nice and uncomplicated without any baggage. Why go looking for trouble?

CHAPTER EIGHT

'SO YOU slept at his place after he'd charged in on his white horse—'

'Harley, actually. Great brute of a thing.'

'His white horse and rescued you,' Beth went on, undeterred by Willow's dry tone. 'And then the guy helps you clean the cottage, invites you back to his place for another great meal—'

'It was Kitty who invited me back, to be strictly truthful.'

'And then turns up the next evening and takes you out to dinner! And you say he's only being neighbourly? Come on, Willow, get real. From what you've told me he isn't some geek or other who's starved for female company and fastens onto the first woman he gets friendly with. The guy's a player, and hot, obviously. And don't wrinkle your nose like that.'

'Well, don't use such terminology, then. You've never even met him.' Willow stared at her sister indignantly. 'A player!'

'Does he or does he not have an active social life?'

'I guess.' She nodded. 'Yes, course he does.'

'And does he give you the impression of being celibate?'

Willow stared helplessly at her sister. Several days had passed since the last meal with Morgan and she had filled them with work, work and more work, staying late at the office and getting in to work early. Arriving home exhausted helped her sleep and prevented endless post-mortems on the hours with Morgan. 'You've got the wrong idea about this,' she said at last. 'Honestly, Beth, you've got totally the wrong idea.'

Beth surveyed her sister over the rim of her mug of hot chocolate. It was Friday lunchtime and Willow had popped in for a quick snack and a chat, although the chat had turned into the third degree for which Beth made no apology. 'So what's the right idea?' she asked, setting her mug down.

She wished she knew, Willow thought ruefully. She didn't know which end of her was up, but she couldn't very well tell Beth that. She didn't want to get involved with a man—any man—but since she'd got to know Morgan better due to the events of last weekend she couldn't get him out of her mind and it was driving her mad. Furthermore, she had been both elated and terrified when he'd turned up last Sunday, worrying all night at the pub that he was going to make a move on her when he saw her home, and then being devastated when he said goodbye with a chaste kiss on her cheek. How was that for inconsistency?

Taking a breath, she said calmly, 'I told you, Beth. Morgan's a neighbour, that's all. A friend. Someone to have a drink with.'

'Has he kissed you?' Then Beth gave a little squeal. 'He has, hasn't he? He's kissed you.'

It was useless to deny it with the flood of hot colour

staining her cheeks. 'Once, with the sort of kiss you mean, and we both agreed it was a mistake and that was the end of that.'

'Was that before or after he turned up on your doorstep and took you to the pub?' Beth asked very intensely.

'Before.' Willow's tone was wary.

'There, you see.' Beth was positively triumphant. 'He came back for more, don't you *see*? Oh, come on, Willow, you must see?'

'Beth, we went for a meal and he saw me home and kissed my cheek as if I was his maiden aunt. If that's passion, I'm a monkey,' said Willow irritably.

'Have a banana, Cheetah.' Beth grinned at her wickedly.

Willow shook her head. 'He didn't ask to see me again and if anything he seemed glad to get away. And I wasn't imagining it,' she added fiercely, as though Beth had contradicted her. 'Anyway, he knows I'm not interested in a relationship and he's not the sort of man to bang his head against a brick wall.'

'So what sort of man is he?' Beth asked gently.

Enigmatically male. Virile. Strong and gentle at the same time, which was dangerously attractive. She could go on for some time because if ever a man was complicated, Morgan was. The way he had listened to her when she'd spoken about her childhood, the hungry look in the beautiful blue eyes… 'Busy,' she said flatly. 'Very busy, with no time to waste.'

Beth cocked an eyebrow sardonically.

'Well, he is.' Willow swallowed the last of her chocolate and stood up. 'I have to be going, thanks for lunch.'

'Pleasure.' Beth reached out and took her hands. 'I'm just going to say one more thing and then I'll shut up.'

Willow eyed her sister apprehensively. She recognised the tone. Whatever Beth was going to say, she wouldn't like it.

'Piers was the biggest mistake you'd ever made in your life and you're incredibly well rid of him,' Beth said steadily. 'But what would be an even bigger mistake is to let him influence the rest of your life in a negative way by shutting yourself away from the prospect of love.' She shook Willow's hands, squeezing them tightly. 'Love might come ten years from now, but it might not. It might be tomorrow. Life isn't guaranteed to come in neat packages when we're ready for it. Just...don't close your mind to anything. That's what I'm saying. Don't miss the opportunity of something great.'

Willow stared at her sister's concerned face through misty eyes and then leant against her for a moment as Beth's arms tightened around her. Beth had spoken as their mother might have done. Then she jerked away, her gaze flashing to Beth's stomach. 'Wow, that was a kick if ever I felt one,' she said in awe. 'Does it often do that?'

'All the time,' Beth said ruefully. 'Especially when I settle down to sleep. Peter's convinced there's a world-class footballer in there. He'll be so surprised if it's a girl.'

They smiled at each other, and after a brief hug Willow left to drive back to work. Much as she loved her sister, she wasn't sorry to leave. The inquisition had been a little rigorous.

Once seated at her desk, however, Willow found melancholy had her in its grip. Feeling the vigorous power of the new life in Beth's stomach had brought home to her yet again all she was going to miss in never having a family of her own. The baby couldn't have known, of course, but it was as though it had been determined to emphasise every word its mother had spoken.

Was she letting Piers influence her even now, subtly control her decisions and her plans for the future? She had never looked at it this way before, but perhaps Beth was right.

The thought panicked her, brought the blood pounding in her ears, and she gasped as though she were drowning.

No, she couldn't risk getting it wrong again. She had thought Piers loved her, that they were going to grow old together with children and grandchildren, that he would protect and cherish her. Instead... She gulped, drawing in much-needed breaths as she willed herself to calm down. Instead she'd placed herself in a living nightmare, the culmination of which had threatened to break her. She couldn't go through that again.

She shut her eyes tightly but she could still see Piers' enraged face on the screen of her mind, hear his curses as he had sent his plate spinning to the floor with a flick of his hand. Such a small thing to signify the end of a marriage—potatoes that were slightly too hard in the centre—but if it hadn't been that it would have been something else. His control over her by that time had been obsessional and she had lived in fear of displeasing him in some way. Her confidence had gone; she'd been a shell of her former self. Piers had told her she was useless in bed and nothing to look at, stupid, dull and boring, and she had believed him. But that night something had snapped and she'd yelled back at him, telling him some home truths that had caught him on the raw.

It had been the first time he had resorted to physical abuse, and when he had hit her she had hit him back, fighting with all her might when he'd laid into her. Their neighbours had called the police and by the time they'd arrived she had been barely conscious, but lucid enough to realise that but for the police's pounding at their door his intention had been to rape her. That knowledge had been the most horrific thing of all.

The divorce had been quick and final and he hadn't even contested it, realising he had gone too far and his hold over her was finished. Her love had turned to hate and he'd known it.

She opened her eyes, staring down at the papers on her desk without seeing them, lost in her dark thoughts. How could something she had thought so good, so fine, have turned out to be so bad, a lie from start to finish? Some months after the divorce one of her friends had told her she'd heard Piers had married again. Someone from his office apparently and, her friend had murmured, the word was Piers had been seeing this girl when he was still married to Willow. She had looked her friend full in the face and told her the girl had her sympathy. And it was true. She had. No one deserved Piers.

Willow sat for a moment more and then her shoulders came back and she straightened. She had work to do. No more thinking. And anyway, Morgan hadn't asked to see her again, she reminded herself, as though that sorted everything out. Which it did, certainly for the immediate future.

She was the last one to leave her particular office at six o'clock although there were still a couple of lights on in other parts of the building when she walked out to the car park after saying goodnight to the security man. The night was windy but dry and she drove home carefully, conscious she was tired, both emotionally and physically. Tomorrow morning she had the chimney sweep coming and she couldn't wait to be able to light a fire in the sitting room again, and in the afternoon the plumber Morgan had recommended was coming to look round the cottage and give her a quote for central heating. Tonight, though, the cottage was cold and faintly damp, and it didn't do anything for her mood as she fixed herself a sandwich and a hot drink in the kitchen. The last few nights she'd gone to bed with a jumper and bedsocks over her pyjamas, and three hot-water bottles positioned at strategic parts of her body.

She went to bed early, once again cocooned like an Eskimo and fell asleep immediately, curled under the duvet like a small animal, waking just before her alarm clock went off at eight. Her nose was cold but the rest of her was as warm as toast and she stretched, willing herself to get out of bed and face the chill.

An hour later she'd washed, dressed and had breakfast and was waiting for the chimney sweep. After a gloomy, rain-filled week the weather had done one of its mercurial transformations. Bright sunshine was spilling through the cottage windows and all was golden light. Her mood, too, had changed. She was in love with her little home again and the future wasn't the black hole she had stared into the night before, but something laced with expectation and hope. Life was good and she was fortunate.

She wasn't sure if she could ever fully trust a man again or take the step Beth had spoken about yesterday, but somehow it didn't seem such an urgent obstacle today but something that would take care of itself. Shrugging at her inconsistency, she made another pot of coffee and was just taking her first sip when a knock came at the front door.

Absolutely sure it was the chimney sweep, she flung

open the door saying, 'Am I pleased to see *you*', and then felt an instant tightening in her stomach as her heart did a somersault.

'Thank you. I didn't expect such a warm welcome.' Morgan was leaning against the door post, his black hair shining in the sunlight and his blue eyes crinkled with a smile.

'I thought you were the chimney sweep,' she said weakly, knowing she'd turned beetroot red. 'I'm waiting for him.'

'Don't spoil it.'

'I— He'll be here in a—a minute.' Oh, for goodness' sake, pull yourself together, she told herself scathingly, hearing her stammer with disgust, but the knowledge had suddenly hit that part of the uplift in her mood had been because there'd been a chance of running into Morgan during the weekend. 'Come in,' she said belatedly, standing aside for him to enter and trying to ignore what the smell of his aftershave did to her senses as he walked past her. 'I've just made some coffee, if you'd like one? And there's toast and preserves in the kitchen.'

'Sounds good.'

Like before he seemed to fill the cottage; the very air seemed to crackle when he was around. Leading the way into the kitchen, she said carefully, 'The guy you recommended for the central heating is coming round this afternoon.' Keep it friendly and informal, nothing heavy, Willow. Don't ask him why he's here, much as you'd like to. 'He seemed very nice on the phone. Very helpful and friendly.'

'Jeff? Yeh, he's a good local contact,' Morgan said a trifle absently. 'He'll do a good job for you.'

'He's just had a cancellation, apparently, and thinks he'd be able to start work this coming week if we agree on a price.'

'That's fortunate. Snap him up and get the job done.'

She turned to face him, an unexpected quiver running through her as she glanced at him standing in the doorway, big and dark and tough-looking. Only somehow she didn't think he was quite as tough as he'd like people to believe, not deep inside. 'White or black?' she asked flatly, not liking the way her thoughts had gone.

'Black,' he said almost impatiently, before adding, 'Thanks.'

After pouring Morgan a coffee she picked up her own and walked over to him, intending they go and sit in the sitting room. Only he didn't move from the doorway, taking his mug but his eyes moving over her face as he murmured, 'I've thought of you all week, do you know that? I've thought of nothing but you.'

Willow stared at him. His tone had been one of self-deprecation, even annoyance, and she didn't know how to respond. Raising her chin slightly, she said, 'Do you expect me to apologise?'

There was a brief silence and then he smiled, humour briefly sparkling in his eyes. 'No, just to listen to me while I explain where I'm coming from. Will you do that?'

She was spared an answer by the real chimney sweep banging on the front door. 'I'll have to let him in.'

He stood for a moment more and then let her through. 'I'll hang around till he goes, if that's OK?'

She turned just before she opened the front door. 'Yes, that's OK,' she said quietly, blessing the fact the turmoil within wasn't evident in her voice.

The next hour was the longest of her life, but eventually Mr George—a burly, red-cheeked man with a wide smile—had removed his covers and other paraphernalia, finished his coffee and cake, and left, and all without making one spot of soot fall on her newly cleaned sitting room. He and Morgan had chatted about local goings-on while he'd worked, and between them they'd eaten most of the cherry cake she'd bought the day before. Willow found she was immensely irritated by the ease with which Morgan had conducted himself, especially because her insides had caught into a giant knot and her heart seemed determined to jump out of her chest every time she looked at him.

The moment the door had closed behind Mr George, Morgan looked straight at her and for a moment she suspected he was as nervous as she was. Then she dismissed the notion. Morgan Wright didn't have a nervous bone in his body.

'So,' he murmured softly as though the last hour hadn't happened and they were continuing their conversation in the kitchen. 'This is the problem as I see it.'

Willow found she didn't like being referred to as a problem. It gave her the strength to stare at him without betraying any emotion and keep her voice steady as she said coolly, 'Problem?'

He'd obviously read her mind and the faintly stern mouth curved upward in a crooked smile. 'Difficulty,' he amended equably. 'We're neighbours. Next-door neighbours,' he added, as though she didn't know. 'Which means the possibility of running into each other now and again is pretty high.'

She didn't agree. He made it sound as though they lived

side by side in a terrace rather than with an acre or two of his grounds separating them, not to mention a high stone wall one way and the lane the other. She opened her mouth to voice this but he didn't give her the chance.

'But that's not really the…difficulty,' he continued. 'There's an attraction between us, you know it and I know it. We enjoy each other's company.' He raised his hand as she went to speak again. 'But here's the problem. Sorry, difficulty. You've just come out of a bad relationship and aren't looking to have a man in your life. Right?'

She nodded, but now she was determined he wasn't going to have this all his own way. 'And you don't do emotional commitment beyond the short-term affair,' she said tightly. 'Which I find…cold-blooded.'

'But you didn't deny there *is* an attraction between us,' he said very quietly, his blue eyes holding hers.

No, she hadn't. She should have, but she hadn't.

He walked to where she was still standing by the front door, not touching her but so close she was enveloped in his body warmth. 'Like I said earlier, I've thought of you all week.' His jaw tensed a few times before he added, 'Awake or asleep. That's not—usual with me.'

He lifted a strand of her hair, letting it shiver through his fingers almost absent-mindedly. 'I'm in London during the week, you're in Redditch, but at the weekends we could see each other sometimes. Nothing heavy, I'm not suggesting I expect you to warm my bed, although you'd be very welcome if so inclined,' he added smokily. 'More than welcome, in fact.'

'I— That—that wouldn't be on the cards.'

He smiled, a sexy quirk that did nothing to quell her

raging hormones. 'I thought not, but bear the invitation in mind,' he murmured lazily. 'It's open-ended.'

He was flirting with her. Willow found the warm fragrance of him was making her legs tremble. And he flirted very well. Obviously plenty of practice, she told herself, danger signals going off loud and strong. 'I—I thought I'd made it clear, I don't want to date. Not after everything that's happened.'

'Oh, you did, you did. Very clear.'

She drew in a deep breath as his fingertips moved against her lower ribs, his palms cupping her sides. It wasn't an aggressive action, just the opposite, but as his strength and vitality flowed through his warm flesh she felt as panic-stricken as if he were making love to her.

'But surely there's nothing wrong in enjoying each other's company now and again?' Morgan continued in a softly cajoling voice that played havoc with her power to reason. 'I expect nothing of you and you expect nothing of me. We can just see how it goes. Take it nice and easy. What do you think?'

She couldn't *think* with him touching her. He was so tough and hard and sexy that the temptation to lay her head against his chest and agree to anything he wanted was strong. She wanted to be looked after, loved, adored, spoilt, all the things she'd made herself say goodbye to for ever long before she and Piers had split. But there was no guarantee a relationship with Morgan would be any better. Piers had been charm itself before he'd married her. She'd learnt the hard way that meant nothing.

She became aware he was studying her with narrowed eyes. 'I'm not your ex-husband,' he said quietly. 'Get that straight in your head, Willow. I like you. I'd like to make love to you, I'm not going to deny it, but I play fair. You know I don't do for ever and that won't change. If friends is all we have, then so be it. You never know, this spark between us might burn itself out in time. What do they say? Familiarity breeds contempt? Togetherness can be a two-edged sword.'

Oh, yes, and Morgan was going to change from the most sexy man on the planet to some kind of a geek, was he? When hell froze over.

She stared into the movie-star-blue eyes and for a moment allowed herself to bathe in the feeling that had been there from the second he'd spoken in the kitchen. A composite of amazement, bewilderment, gratification, delight and sheer shock that this tough, enigmatic, wealthy and intelligent man, who also happened to be deliciously attractive to boot, was interested in *her*.

'You mentioned we live next door to each other,' she said weakly. 'What if it ends badly? Wouldn't that make things awkward?'

'It won't.' He kissed the tip of her nose lightly.

'You might meet someone.' The world was full of lovely women.

'I meet people all the time, Willow,' he said gently.

'A woman, someone who's free to get involved...properly. Who wants what you want.' Even now she found it difficult to say; what would it be like if it actually happened after she'd been seeing him for a while? She shouldn't be considering this.

He didn't deny it. 'Friendship can survive worse than that.'

She couldn't think of anything worse than that right at this moment but didn't think it prudent to say so.

'Decision time.' He pulled her closer into him, but this time he took her mouth in a kiss that nipped at her lower lip before deepening into an erotic assault on her senses. Warmth spread through her as his mouth left hers and trailed over her cheek, then her throat, before returning to her lips in a swift final kiss. He stepped back a pace, letting go of her, and she felt the loss in every fibre of her being. 'So?' he said levelly, face expressionless. 'What's it to be?'

'You said no lovemaking,' she protested weakly.

'I said I didn't expect you to jump into bed with me,' he corrected gently. 'I didn't say anything about kissing or cuddling or a whole host of other...pleasant things between friends. And that's all that was, nothing heavy.'

'You kiss all your friends like that?'

His eyes were deep pools of laughter. 'Only those with honey-coloured, spicy skin, green eyes and red hair.'

There were a hundred and one reasons why she shouldn't get mixed up with Morgan Wright, be it as a 'friend' or anything else, not least because absolutely nothing could come of it and she might end up getting hurt. She stared at him, her mind racing. But guidelines *had* been drawn—albeit somewhat fuzzy ones if that kiss was anything to go by. And why shouldn't she just go out and enjoy herself sometimes with a male companion? She was still young, for goodness' sake, and free, and she knew what—and what *not*—she was getting into with Morgan. He might be able to charm the birds out of the trees, but he *had* been honest with her. She knew exactly where she stood with Morgan. Didn't she?

Willow could still smell a lingering scent of lime from his aftershave and although he hadn't ravished her mouth her lips were tingling. He was disturbingly good at this kissing business.

Could she bear to say no, to effectively wipe him out of her life for good? He wasn't the type of man to beg.

She took a deep breath. 'I see nothing wrong in us getting to know each other better. It's—it's nice to know there's a friend around if you need one,' she added primly.

'Very nice,' he agreed gravely. 'Great, in fact.'

'And the cottage is a little remote. If I need a neighbour in an emergency—'

'You can call on me, any time of the day or—' he paused briefly '—night.'

'Quite,' she said briskly, taking his words at face value and ignoring the innuendo. 'Which is reassuring for a single woman.'

His smile this time was merely a twitch, but the piercing blue eyes glimmered with laughter. She wondered if he knew how that incredible, deep, bright blueness could hold you spellbound. Then she answered herself wryly. Of course he knew. And she was going to have to be very careful to resist Morgan's particular brand of magic.

This was nothing more than a brief interlude for him, a diverting game even. She'd caught his interest more because of what she wasn't than what she was. Unwittingly her refusal to fall into bed with him had singled her out as something of a challenge; it was the age-old scenario of the thrill of the chase.

But as long as she knew all that and kept it very firmly to the forefront of her mind, she could do this. And she wanted to do it. She wanted to get to know Morgan better, to find out what made him tick. She wanted to discover more about his past, what had made him the tough, cynical man he had become. To understand his work, what motivated him. He was a fascinating individual, she admitted it. Magnetic even. He had a quality that drew people into his orbit almost in spite of themselves. And she wanted to be with him…for a while.

She had been totally straight with him; he knew she had no intention of sleeping with him. That being the case, she had nothing to lose. Nothing at all. Did she?

CHAPTER NINE

WILLOW and Morgan ate at a little restaurant tucked away in a small market town some twenty miles away that night. When he arrived at the cottage he was driving the Aston Martin and the beautiful car added to the worries that had crowded in the minute he'd left. Morgan was way, way out of her league, she told herself as he helped her into the passenger seat and shut the door quietly, the doubts that had been rampant since the morning crowding in. Seeing him like this was going against everything she'd decided for the future on breaking with Piers. How could she be so stupid, so fickle? This was such a mistake.

Contrary to her fears at the beginning of the evening, they enjoyed a night of easy talk and easy laughter, and when Morgan dropped her home he declined her offer of a nightcap and left her on the doorstep with a firm, confident kiss that kept her warm until she was in bed.

The next day Kitty cooked Sunday lunch for them and they took the dogs for a long walk in the surrounding countryside in the afternoon, talking the whole time—about his work, hers, plays and films they'd seen and books they'd read. Nothing too deep and nothing too personal.

She didn't stay for tea, saying she'd brought some work home to do, which wasn't true, and that she had to move stuff in the cottage so Jeff could start work in the morning, which was true.

By the next weekend Jeff had finished the job and the cottage was blissfully warm. Willow had never realised until the last couple of weeks what a perfectly wonderful invention radiators were, and she found herself touching them in thankfulness every time she passed. They'd transformed her home.

Beth invited herself and Peter for Saturday lunch on the excuse they wanted to drop in her housewarming present—a lovely stone birdbath for the garden—although Willow was fully aware her sister was hoping to see Morgan. She'd told Beth she was seeing Morgan occasionally—as friends, she'd emphasised—and Beth had been instantly agog but she'd resisted saying more.

She hadn't mentioned Beth's visit to Morgan when he'd phoned her in the week to invite her out to dinner on Saturday night. She didn't want him to think she was hinting he come and meet her sister, or that he stay away—depending on which way he took it—and neither did she want Beth forming an opinion about Morgan yet. If they met and Beth thought he was the bee's knees that would create one set of potential problems, and conversely if her sister and Peter didn't take to Morgan that would cause difficulty in another way. No, it was far better to maintain the status quo for the time being.

Saturday turned out to be the sort of mellow English autumn day that inspired poets to pen the odd sonnet or two, and after lunch it was warm enough to take their coffee into the garden and sit on the ancient wooden benches she'd uncovered in the midst of what had been a jungle.

The trees surrounding the garden were now clothed in a mantle of gold, bronze and orange, the sky was a bright cloudless blue and a host of birds were twittering and squabbling and enjoying the sunshine. They watched as a robin, braver than the rest of its feathered kind, explored the new bird bath, which Willow had filled earlier. He had a great time splashing around.

'This is lovely.' Beth breathed in the air, one hand resting on the swell of her stomach. 'So peaceful.'

They sat for a long time idly chatting, and when Beth dozed off with her head resting on Peter's shoulder and he whispered she'd been awake most of the night due to the baby deciding it was football practice, Willow fetched a warm throw from the house to tuck around her sister and then sat listening to Peter's plans for the baby's future, which seemed to revolve around his favourite football club.

The gentle shadows of dusk had been encroaching for some time when Willow glanced surreptitiously at her watch. Morgan was due to arrive at seven and it was getting late. She fetched Peter another coffee, making sure she was none too quiet about it, but Beth didn't stir. After another twenty minutes she threw diplomacy to the wind. 'I'm going out at seven,' she said, when Peter refused the offer of more coffee, 'and don't you think it's getting chilly out here now the light's all but gone?'

Peter smiled blithely. 'We're fine,' he said, tucking the throw more securely round his sleeping wife, 'but don't let me stop you getting ready.'

Men! She loved her brother-in-law and she couldn't

think of a better husband for Beth or father for their child, but right at that moment she could have kicked him. Somewhat helplessly, she tried again. 'I'd hate for you to get bitten. I noticed a couple of mosquitos earlier.'

'I never get bitten and there's not much of Beth visible under this rug. Besides, she needs the sleep,' he said fondly.

Great. Just great. She marched into the house.

Half an hour later she'd showered and dressed in the new, deceptively simple frock she'd bought that week, a demure, sleeveless, jade-green number, which was high-necked and slim-fitting but with a naughtily high slit up one side. Her hair, shining like silk thanks to a wickedly expensive conditioner, was looped on the back of her head and she was wearing the long jade earrings her parents had bought her for her birthday just before the accident, which were infinitely precious for that reason.

She stared at herself in the mirror. She had been so demoralised during the years with Piers, so crushed and ashamed, so angry with herself for letting him hurt her over and over again but unable to rise above the control he'd exerted, that she'd forgotten what it felt like to dress up for a man who desired her. For the first time in what seemed like aeons she was pulling out all the stops and dressing to impress.

Panic sliced through her, undoing the elusive moments of pleasure she'd felt at her reflection.

Forcing herself to breathe deeply, she shut her eyes for a few moments. The emotional claustrophobia that reared its head at the thought of involvement was a legacy of her marriage and nothing more, she told herself grimly. It wasn't even connected to Morgan, not really. It could be any man taking her out tonight and she would feel the same way. The feeling of walking into a trap, of losing her freedom and independence could be overcome. Beth had said she was letting Piers still influence her life and that had rankled ever since. Because—she opened her eyes and stared at herself again, her mouth rueful—it was true. So she had to master this feeling and herself.

'Wow! You look a million dollars.'

She hadn't heard Beth come up the stairs and now she swung round to face her sister, smiling at the expression on her face. 'It's only me,' she said with an embarrassed giggle.

'You look fantastic.' Beth was grinning like a Cheshire cat. 'Absolutely fantastic. So, this going out is a date with Morgan, I take it?' She plonked herself down happily on the bed.

Prevarication was out of the question. Willow nodded.

'And you want us to get out of your hair?'

Willow smiled. 'You're prepared to make the ultimate sacrifice?' she said lightly. 'Greater love hath no sister…'

'Grudgingly.' Beth laughed. 'What time's he coming?'

The knock at the front door was answer enough. They heard Peter open the door, the murmur of male voices and then Peter called, 'Willow? Morgan's here.'

'Sorry.' Beth's voice was apologetic but her eyes were sparkling with delight. 'Looks like it's too late to escape.'

'I won't be a minute,' Willow called down, before eyeing her sister severely. 'No third degree, OK?'

'I wouldn't dream of it.' Beth managed to look shocked.

'Course you wouldn't.' Willow sighed. Her worst nightmare.

When they entered the sitting room the two men were standing with a drink in their hands deep in conversation. Willow's heart stopped, then bounded when she caught sight of Morgan. As always, he looked bigger and tougher and sexier than she remembered. 'Hi,' she said, faintly.

'Hi, yourself,' he said very softly, intimately.

He smiled and the sun came up, or that was how it seemed. 'You've met Peter,' she said, relieved at how calm she sounded. 'And this is my sister, Beth. Beth, Morgan Wright.'

'Nice to meet you, Beth.' Morgan held out his hand and Beth took it after one swift glance at Willow, which was all too eloquent. Tasty didn't do this man justice.

OK, Willow told herself wryly. Hadn't she known all along it would be the bee's-knees reaction? What woman could resist him?

She listened to Beth gabbling that they were so-o-o sorry they'd delayed Willow, but they were leaving right now and it was so-o-o nice to have met Willow's friend, whom they'd heard so much about.

OK, Willow thought. Stop right there, Beth.

Morgan's whole face was smiling now. 'Likewise,' he said warmly, 'but do you have to rush back straight away? Why don't you join us for dinner? We'd love that, wouldn't we, Willow?'

Willow saw Beth's eyes widen. Game, set and match to Morgan, she thought resignedly. In one fell swoop he'd won her sister for ever. He was good. He was very, very good.

Beth did the 'Oh, we couldn't possibly' thing very well, but Willow could tell her sister's heart wasn't in it. Within a short while she was seated beside Morgan in the Aston Martin and Beth and Peter were following behind in their faithful old Cavalier. She sat feeling a little shell-shocked.

'You didn't mind?' Morgan asked after a moment or two.

'You inviting Beth and Peter to join us? No, not at all,' she lied smoothly. 'Why would I mind?' Why, indeed?

'Peter had mentioned they'd come for lunch and with it being seven o'clock and Beth not having eaten since, in her condition, you know…' He gave her stiff face a swift glance.

Willow flushed. The reprimand was gentle and covert, but it felt like a reprimand nonetheless. 'I said I didn't mind.'

'Good.' Another moment or two slipped by. 'You look incredible, by the way,' he said softly. 'Absolutely beautiful.'

Her flush deepened. 'Thank you.' Charmer!

'And I'd much rather have been alone with you tonight.'

In spite of the fact she knew full well she was being sweet-talked by an expert, Willow found herself melting. It took all her willpower to ignore the sensual quality to his voice and say evenly, 'With the baby coming soon Beth won't have too many opportunities for spur-of-the-moment nights out.'

'No, I guess that's right,' he replied.

'I presume wherever it is we're going can stretch a table for two to four?' she asked crisply.

'Oh, yes.' He nodded. 'They're very accommodating.'

'Good. No problem, then.' She stared out of the window.

A mile or two slipped by before he murmured, 'What, exactly, had Beth heard about me, by the way?' Laughter in his voice.

'That was just social etiquette,' she said a mite too quickly.

'Social etiquette? Ah, yes. I see.' He gave an understanding nod.

'Like your reply,' she said stiffly.

'But I *had* heard plenty about your sister, Willow,' he reminded her gently.

She supposed he had. Beth and Peter and their life

together had seemed fairly innocuous a subject on the walk last weekend. Deciding attack was the best defence, she said testily, 'Why do you always have to have the last word, Morgan Wright?'

'A definite character fault,' he agreed gravely.

She suddenly laughed; she couldn't help it. 'I've made Beth promise not to ask you if you can keep me in the manner to which I've become accustomed, but if she goes into parent mode you'll have to excuse her. Her hormones are all over the place at the moment. And being happily married she thinks that is the only way anyone can be truly happy in life.' She wrinkled her nose.

'And you? What do you think?' he said quietly.

'Me?' She had to force the laugh now. 'Like you, I think it's a recipe for disaster.'

Morgan made no comment to this. 'She's a lot like you.'

'In looks? Yes, I suppose so. And we're both like our mum.'

He glanced at her, a swift look, but said no more for some miles. It was as they drew into the grounds of a large hotel he said quietly, 'I've missed you this week. Have you missed me?'

Light words came to mind, words that could have passed off the moment without betraying anything of herself. Instead she said just as quietly, 'Yes.'

The four of them got on so well the evening flew by on wings. Willow really did think Beth would have followed them home but for Peter putting his foot down where they made their goodbye in the hotel car park. 'Say goodbye nicely,' he prompted.

'Sorry.' Beth was giggly as she whispered into Willow's ear as she hugged her goodnight. It certainly wasn't due to the sparkling water she'd consumed all night due to her condition, Willow reflected with a smile. 'But I've *so* enjoyed this evening. He's gorgeous—Morgan, I mean. And we didn't expect him to treat us, you know. The pair of you must come round for a meal soon, promise? We'd love to have you before the baby comes.'

'Peter's waiting,' Willow pointed out gently.

'Don't freeze him out, Willow.' Beth wasn't giggly any longer. 'Give it a chance. He's gorgeous, he really is.'

'Beth, neither of us want anything serious. This is just a few meals out together, a little fling, that's all.' She hugged Beth again and then stepped away from her, becoming aware as she did so that Morgan was closer than she'd thought, close enough, maybe, to hear what she'd said, even though he was talking to Peter. For a moment she felt awful, then her chin lifted. She hadn't said anything out of place. It *was* what they'd agreed. He'd been the one to suggest it, not her.

Morgan put his arm round her waist as they waved the others off. For a second the sense of déjà vu was so strong she felt sick. How many times had Piers stood with her like this, playing the devoted husband after Beth and Peter had left them after an evening together? Whispering into her hair that the meal had been a shambles, she'd laughed too much, she hadn't laughed enough, her dress was all wrong or she was putting on too much weight, and all the time disguising his poison with a tender smile.

'What's the matter? Do you feel ill?'

Morgan's voice brought her face jerking to meet his and

she saw he was looking at her with concern. Shakily she shook her head. 'I'm fine.' She attempted a smile, which didn't come off.

'You're as white as a sheet and far from fine,' he said roughly. 'What's wrong? Have I said something?'

'It's nothing to do with you—with tonight, I mean.' She took a deep breath; she was saying this all wrong. 'What I mean is, I've enjoyed tonight. I thought the four of us got on great.'

'Something reminded you of him again, didn't it?' It was as though he could read her mind at times. 'Something I did? Is that it? Tell me so I don't make the same mistake again.'

'No. Yes. Oh—' she shook her head, stepping away from him and beginning to walk to the car in a corner of the car park '—can we forget it?' She didn't want to do the Piers thing again.

He opened the car door for her and helped her in, shutting the door and walking round the bonnet with a grim face. Once he was seated, he turned to her. The muted lighting in the car park was enough for her to see he wasn't going to let the matter drop. 'Tell me,' he said very quietly. 'Please.'

'There's nothing to tell.' She felt hemmed in, trapped.

'Little fling or not, you *will* tell me, Willow, if we have to sit here all night.' He wasn't angry and his voice was soft.

So he had heard. Woodenly, she said, 'Piers used to put his arm round me like that when we said goodbye to family or friends, that's all.'

He swore softly before he said, 'And?'

'And?' she prevaricated, not wanting to say more.

'From the little you've told me about this cowboy there is definitely an and.' He reached out and lifted her chin so she was forced to meet his eyes. 'Tell me,' he said again, but this time with such tenderness she found she had to clench every muscle in her body against the urge to cry. 'I don't want to make any more mistakes that can put that look on your face.'

'I told you, it wasn't you.' She lowered her head again, smoothing her dress over her knees with small jerky movements. 'Piers was a control freak,' she whispered after a moment or two. 'I suppose the signs were there before we got married but I was too inexperienced to recognise them. Maybe we'd never have married if my parents hadn't died, I don't know.' She shrugged wearily. 'But we did marry and within a little while he'd turned into someone else. He—he built himself up by knocking me down. Not physically, at least not until the end, but he'd make me feel stupid, worthless, ugly.'

Morgan's hand covered one of hers. She could feel his anger.

'We'd stand like we stood tonight and all the time he'd keep up a litany of what I'd done wrong, how embarrassing I was, how people felt sorry for him because he was with me. It—it was just now and again at first and he said he was pointing out things for my own good, because he loved me so much. Then it got more and more—' She stopped abruptly. 'But to everyone else, even Beth, he appeared the loving husband. After I left him she said she'd known something was wrong but she thought I was still grieving for Mum and Dad.'

'You didn't confide in her?' he asked quietly. 'Not even Beth?'

She shook her head. 'I can't believe I didn't now, but at

the time…' She shook her head again. 'He made me believe I was in the wrong. He—he was very clever.'

'I can think of a better word to describe him.' He reached out and smoothed a strand of hair from her cheek. 'What made you finally break his control?'

She looked at him. Yes, that was exactly what she had done, she thought with an element of surprise. At the time she'd looked on her leaving him as an escape, a feral, self-preservation thing, but it was more than that. The night she had fought back with everything she had—spirit, soul and body—something *had* been broken. She might have been left emotionally and physically battered, but it had been her who had won. She had become herself again that night, albeit an older, wiser self.

'He went too far,' she said flatly. 'Much too far.'

'Don't tell me if you don't want to.'

She thought for a moment. Did she want to? There was an unsettling blend of tenderness and anger in the tough male face and she knew the anger wasn't directed against her. Something melted. 'He threw his dinner on the floor. It wasn't the first time but that night something in me snapped…'

She told him it all, even the fact that towards the end of their fight she'd known he intended to violate her, which had brought a strength she hadn't known she was capable of. She wasn't aware she was trembling until he leaned across and pulled her into him, one arm holding her close as he rested his chin on the silk of her hair. 'I would give all I own for five minutes alone with this man. He'd never touch another woman again.'

His voice had been soft but of a quality that brought her

head up as her eyes sought his. What she saw in his face made her say quickly, 'It's all right. *I'm* all right. I am, really.'

'Are you?' The blue eyes were piercingly direct and she found she couldn't break their hold.

She had to swallow hard before she said, 'Of course.'

'For something like this there is no "of course".'

A long pause ensued but their gazes didn't unlock. She wondered why it was that this man, a man she hadn't known until a short while ago, seemed to understand how deeply she had been affected by Piers' cruelty when most of her friends had expected her to bounce back within weeks or certainly a few months. Hesitantly, she whispered, 'I'm getting there but—'

'What?' His gaze didn't waver. 'What's the but?'

'I never want to give the control of my life over to someone else again,' she said with total honesty.

For a moment he continued to stare at her, then a slight twist of a smile touched his lips. 'It scares the hell out of me too,' he admitted huskily, his mouth falling on hers. His lips were warm and firm and as hers opened instinctively beneath them his tongue probed the corner or her mouth, teasing her, coaxing a response she was powerless to resist. The kiss changed to one of infinite hunger and she heard him groan, a half-irritated groan at the limitations within the car as he tried to move closer and was restricted by the controls.

He raised his head, faint amusement in his voice as he murmured, 'I haven't done this for years and now I remember why. You need to be a contortionist.'

Aiming to match his tone, she said, 'You haven't kissed a girl?'

His laugh was a deep rumble. 'Made out in a car. The

idea's good but the reality is less than practical.' The blue eyes held hers. 'Coffee at your place?'

Aware that something vital had changed in the last minutes she felt a yearning that cut through all her carefully thought-out guidelines for the future. 'Yes,' she whispered. Crazy, madness even, but yes.

CHAPTER TEN

THEY said very little on the drive back from the hotel. Morgan was aware he was driving on automatic, every part of himself tuned into the woman sitting so calm and still beside him. She appeared poised and composed, dispassionate even.

The calmness was a façade. He knew it as surely as drawing in the next breath. Willow had said she didn't want a permanent relationship. Well, neither did he. Not a relationship that came with a whole load of conditions at least. So why did her honesty grate so much? And it did. Hell, it did.

She was as tense as a coiled spring behind that composed exterior. *He knew it.* He took a bend much too fast and as the tyres squealed warned himself to concentrate. The anger he felt towards the ex-husband who'd left her so painfully damaged was growing, not diminishing. He wanted to make things right for her, to convince her she was a beautiful, sexy, gorgeous woman whom any man would count himself lucky to have in his arms. That was what he wanted. Because it was true.

Oh, yeah? His conscience wouldn't let him get away

with it. So this had nothing to do with the fact he'd wanted to make love to her from the first time he'd seen her tending that damn silly bonfire, all smudged and tousled and deliciously bewildered? The gnawing hunger for her body had been with him for night after torturous night, that was the truth of it. She'd stormed into his dreams every time he'd laid his head on the pillow and resolutely stayed there no matter how many cold showers he'd taken. And he had taken plenty.

OK, OK. He made mental acknowledgement to his desire. But a good healthy sex life between a man and a woman couldn't be anything but satisfying for both of them, could it? Damn it, it was what made the world go round, after all.

And what about all his protestations of friendship and letting matters develop at their own pace? Did he genuinely think she was ready for this? Emotionally, where it counted with a woman?

His thoughts went round and round in his head and when he reached the lane leading to his house and Willow's cottage he had to admit he had no clear recollection of the journey from the hotel. He parked on the grass verge outside her garden gate, walking round the bonnet and helping her out of the car without saying a word. She looked slender and delicate, vulnerable.

'You're beautiful.' As he took her in his arms in the dark shadows the tenseness in her shoulders became apparent. He drew her closer, dropping little kisses on her hair and forehead until she slowly relaxed against him with a breath of a sigh. Her hands had been small fists against his chest but now her fingers uncurled and crept down to his waist as her body curved closer into his.

He let his mouth caress her cheeks, her nose, her ears with the same small kisses, making no demands. 'You're beautiful,' he murmured again before taking her mouth in a deeper kiss, his hands falling to her hips as he brought her softness against the hard evidence of his arousal. 'So very beautiful…'

He could feel her slowly relaxing minute by minute and for some time he contented himself with exploring the sweetness of her mouth, bringing all his control to bear to prevent himself crushing her against him. If he hadn't known she had been married he would have thought he was dealing with a virgin by the nervousness he was sensing; it was further proof of just how badly her ex-husband had hurt her.

The night was cool but not cold and the darkness was scented with the faint aroma of hedgerows and wood-smoke. Somewhere in the distance an owl hooted but Morgan's world had shrunk down to the woman in his arms. He wanted her, he thought with an ache in his loins that was painful, but he wanted more than her body. He could hardly remember this feeling; it had been a long time since Stephanie when he'd thought he'd been in love and wanted to know every little thing about a woman.

Women abounded in London, beautiful and intelligent women who were self-confident without being egotistical and who knew their way round their own needs and what they wanted from a man. They were single by choice and intended to remain that way and he had found that suited him just fine. But somehow Willow was different and he couldn't figure out why.

Then she kissed him back with an unmistakable hunger that threatened his slow and easy approach. He tugged her more securely into the cradle of his hips as her arms wound around his neck, her hands sliding into the thickness of his hair. He covered her lips with his in a kiss that held nothing back, probing, sipping, tasting as a deep hunger and explosive warmth enveloped them both. His hips ground against hers as one hand positioned itself in the small of her back, the other cupping the fullness of one breast through the soft fabric of her dress.

He heard her catch her breath as she arched against him and the evidence of her pleasure intensified his, the knowledge that she wanted him as badly as he wanted her electrifying.

This time his kiss was so demanding it was almost a kind of consummation, as though she were accepting the thrust of him inside her body and he didn't try to soften his claim. Slowly, erotically, his fingertips began a sensual rhythm on her breast until she was trembling against him, little moans escaping her throat. She felt fluid, like warm raw silk.

He could take her inside right now and do anything he wanted to her; she was his for the taking. The usual thrill of conquest was there but there was a strange feeling of something being missing. Or wrong. Yes, definitely wrong.

He lifted his head, inhaling deeply and audibly as he tried to focus on what his mind was telling him rather than the savagely strong, primal urge of his body.

If he took her to bed now he would be as guilty of manipulating her as that sick so-and-so she'd married.

He looked down at her in his arms. She was breathing raggedly, her eyes still closed and her delicious mouth half open, her swollen lips bearing evidence of their lovemaking. Desire sliced through him as viciously as the blade of a knife and he tensed against the bittersweet potency of it, even as the intensity of what he was feeling provided its own sobering check on his libido.

He was a man, not an animal. He had mastery over his physical needs, not the other way round. After what Willow had gone through she needed to be sure of what she was doing when she opened up her mind and her body to intimacy again, and he knew full well he had used his sexual experience to sweep away her defences tonight. *She was too beautiful, too special, to hurt.*

The few seconds when she kept her eyes shut enabled him to compose his features even though he felt as though he'd been punched in the stomach by the strength of that last thought. He'd been right all along—he should have listened to the small, still voice of sanity, which had told him getting involved with this woman would be a gigantic mistake. Looking back, he'd known deep inside he was falling in love with her even then. And now it was too late. He totally and irrevocably loved her.

'Morgan?'

There was bewilderment as well as desire in the green eyes when he met her gaze, and he held her close for a moment more before straightening and steadying her as he stepped back a pace. 'I'm sorry,' he said softly. 'That wasn't part of the deal, was it?' Nor had been falling in love with her.

She blinked before shaking her head, whether in affirmation of what he'd said or confusion he wasn't sure.

He stared at her, knowing he had to make one thing perfectly clear after what her ex-husband had put her through. 'I want to make love to you, Willow,' he said quietly, 'more than I've ever wanted before with anyone else. I eat, sleep, breathe you half the time and the other half I'm taking cold showers. Nothing works. I feel you're in my blood and my bones, let alone my head.'

He watched her assimilate what he'd said, her eyes searching his face as though to verify the truth of it.

'But tonight isn't the night, is it?' he continued huskily. 'It's too soon. Tomorrow you wouldn't be able to handle what'd happened and you'd be hard on yourself.'

She hooked a strand of hair behind her ear and gave a nervous half-laugh. 'I don't know what you mean.'

'I think you do.' He reached out and lightly touched her forehead as he said, 'What goes on in here is different to what your body is crying out for. The two have to agree.'

She was holding herself very straight now, her features tight as though she dared not let any expression show. 'You're very sure of yourself, aren't you?' she said, but her voice shook. 'Very sure you know what's right and wrong for me.'

'I have to be.' He kept his voice even and low. 'For your sake and mine too. I've never taken a woman who wasn't one hundred per cent sure she wanted it as much as I did, and I don't intend to start with you.' *Especially with you.* 'I don't want to hurt you, Willow. Intentionally or unintentionally, I don't want that.'

She turned her head away as though she couldn't bear to look at him. 'I'm not a child, Morgan,' she said tightly.

'Believe me, of that I am well aware.'

'And I wouldn't allow myself to be hurt by anyone again.'

He was silent until she raised her head and met his eyes again. 'That one sentence says it all,' he said softly. 'If you'd have said you are prepared to take the risk of being hurt again, that life is all about taking chances, that you were at a stage where you understood you didn't want to be standing on the touchline looking at life but entering in, I'd have felt you were ready. As it is, those barriers are still ten feet high, aren't they?'

This time the silence stretched longer. 'Who are you to talk?' she said after a full ten seconds had ticked by. 'You told me yourself you got your fingers burnt years ago and from then on decided no long-term commitment but just a series of affairs would do. You said you didn't want more than that.'

He nodded. 'Yes, I did. And the pleasure of a beautiful woman's body in bed and a mind that is stimulating and intelligent has been enough for me.' Until now. 'But you aren't like that, Willow. *You* told *me* that. So I come back to where I started and it's that you have to be sure in your head as well as your body what you want. No one can make that happen but you.'

Even in the darkness he could see her cheeks were warm. 'So why did you…?'

Her voice trailed away but the question was clear. Morgan thought about prevaricating, even lying. He didn't want to sound the final death knell on this relationship that wasn't a relationship, but having come this far… 'I wanted to sleep with you tonight because wanting you the way I do is sweet torture,' he said evenly. 'But in the final analysis I knew I couldn't look myself in the eyes when I shave tomorrow morning if I'd seduced you. You said you're not a child and you're absolutely right. You're a woman, and one who needs to know her own mind when, and if, you take that decision. If I'd continued we both know I would have been taking that away from you. Once it was over you would have regretted sleeping with me tonight. Am I right?' He stared into the green eyes steadily.

She stared back, an unreadable expression in her gaze. 'I don't know if this is a clever ploy to convince me I can trust you,' she said at last.

Anger bit. His jaw clenched and he forced himself to relax and keep his tone steady. 'That's something you'll have to work out for yourself.' He stepped backwards and away from the temptation of her. 'Kitty's expecting you for Sunday lunch. Do I tell her you're coming?' he added flatly.

A pause. She still continued to look at him, unmoving.

His heart thumped like a gong in his chest and he couldn't seem to regulate his breathing. He had no idea how she'd react.

'As friends?' she asked quietly after what seemed like a lifetime. 'We're still talking friends here?'

He looked her straight in the eyes. 'What else?'

She smiled wanly. 'If you still want me to after tonight.'

The need to take her in his arms again was fierce, but this time the desire was to comfort and protect. Softly, he said, 'Willow, I've been honest with you. I want you, you know that, but if we continue as friends and that's all there is, so be it.'

Her mouth trembled for just a second; then she turned away. 'That will be all there is,' she said with an air of finality. 'So do you still want me to come for lunch?'

He felt his temper starting to come alive again but something deep inside told him it was imperative he didn't let it show. But he wasn't going to beg. 'Like I said, that's something you'll have to work out for yourself.'

She had reached her front door and he watched her

insert the key in the lock before she turned to face him again. Before she could speak, he said, 'Goodnight, Willow. Sleep well,' and turned from the sight of her.

He was actually half in the car when she shouted, 'What time is lunch?'

Over his shoulder, he called casually, 'One or thereabouts. And bring boots and a waterproof coat; we'll be walking the dogs in the afternoon.' And without waiting for a reply he shut the car door and started the engine. By the time he had done a three-point turn there was no sign of her.

He stopped the car just before the turn into his drive and sat in the darkness, trying to get his head round what had just happened. His emotions were in turmoil and for the life of him he didn't know if he had just made the best or the worst decision of his life. One thing he did know. He loved her. And loving her he had to let her go to either love him back one day or walk away from him.

He continued to sit for a long time and when he finally started the car again, his face was damp.

CHAPTER ELEVEN

WILLOW was painfully nervous when Morgan opened the door to her the next day. He'd called her mobile phone earlier that morning to see if she was all right and the conversation had been stilted, at least on her part, she admitted miserably. Morgan had seemed his usual cool, faintly amused self. But then he probably hadn't tossed and turned the night away before finally giving up any thoughts of sleep as dawn broke. He was a man after all, she thought viciously, and they were a different species. Logical, cold, control freaks. Only Morgan wasn't like that and she knew it. Or did she? She'd thought Piers was the genuine article, hadn't she? Not exactly ten out of ten there, then.

So the arguments had gone round and round in her head until it was actually a relief when lunchtime approached and she went to face the wolf in his lair. Or that was what it felt like.

'Hi.' He was smiling with his eyes as well as his mouth as he opened the door to her, and before she could protest he'd kissed her swiftly on the mouth before taking her coat. 'Come and have a drink,' he said easily once she'd finished fussing the dogs. 'Sherry, wine or one of my famous cocktails?'

It was impossible to remain on edge for long; Morgan had a witty and slightly wicked sense of humour and within a short time she was laughing at something he'd said and the atmosphere had diffused. By the time he saw her home under a moonlit sky things were back to normal.

Or were they? Willow asked herself later that night, curled up in bed but wide awake in spite of the sleepless hours the night before. Like it or not, their relationship had gone a little deeper, moved up a gear, call it what you would. He'd kissed her warmly on the doorstep but hadn't prolonged the contact, taking the key from her fingers and opening the door for her as the kiss ended, and pushing her gently into the house as he'd blown her one last kiss before shutting the door. She had stood immobile for some moments, overwhelmed by such mixed feelings she wouldn't have been able to name any one as uppermost. Regret, longing, confusion, relief, but overall a curious kind of restlessness, which was compounded by the fact she wouldn't see Morgan for another five days.

And she wanted to see him. A rush of longing swept through her, intensifying to a physical ache as she stared into the quiet darkness. How would she feel if he suddenly said he didn't want to see *her* any more? If he'd had enough of this 'friendship'?

She clenched her muscles against the rawness of the thought, then forced herself to slowly relax. She'd cope, she'd survive. She'd got through the break-up of her marriage, hadn't she? And nothing could be worse than that.

Really? Her mind seemed determined to play devil's

advocate. Was she sure about that? Had Piers ever stirred her inner self in the way Morgan did? Piers had been like a beautifully wrapped gift that turned out to be an empty box, worthless and of no lasting value. Morgan, on the other hand, was like tough brown paper done up with string, which held something priceless inside.

The thought shocked her and she sat bolt upright in bed, telling herself she was being ridiculous. Her heart was pounding and there was a lump in her throat, the feeling that she wanted to cry uppermost. Her head was trying to tell her something.

If only he had swept her off her feet last night—literally—and carried her inside and up to bed and made love to her all night so the decision wasn't hers. That was what most men would have done in his place. Then it would have been a fait accompli. No going back.

But Morgan's dead right, isn't he? the nasty little voice pointed out. If he'd done that she would have felt terrible in the cold light of day and probably hated him as much as she loved him. *Loved* him? Where on earth had that come from?

Her body went rigid. *She didn't love him.* She hugged herself, shivering, but the chill was within. She did not love Morgan Wright. She wouldn't be so monumentally foolish as to fall in love with a man who had made it clear from the outset that he wasn't interested in permanency or for ever or anything remotely approaching it. A man who conducted his lovelife with a ruthless determination to stay clear of the trap of matrimony.

Willow sat for long minutes, her head whirling, and when she slid down under the covers again she gave a short mirthless laugh. She had to be the most stupid woman on the planet. How could she have gone from the frying pan into the fire? She had loved one man who had turned out to be so, so wrong; how could she have fallen for another who was equally wrong, if for different reasons? This couldn't be happening.

What was she going to do? She lay, fighting for composure and telling herself she was not—she was *not*—going to cry. He didn't know how she felt and she hadn't, *thank goodness*, made the fatal mistake of sleeping with him, which would have complicated things further. She was his weekend 'friend'; she had no idea what he got up to in the week and she didn't want to know. She had to face the fact she was only on the perimeter of his life and that when this desire for her body he had spoken of began to fade, most likely their weekend dates would become less and less. And that was OK, it really was. It had to be.

Over the next few weeks this resolve was tested. Morgan had taken to calling her now and again in the evenings; pleasant, warm, amiable calls, which sometimes lasted as long as an hour. He'd ask her how she was and what she'd been doing before telling her about his day, putting an amusing slant on his conversation, which often had her giggling helplessly. And the weekends—oh, the weekends… He took her to the theatre and to the cinema; dancing at a couple of nightclubs in the first big town some distance away from the cottage, and for some delicious meals out. Other times they'd dine at his home, watch TV or listen to music, and take the dogs for long walks when the weather permitted.

On her birthday in October he whisked her off to a

superb restaurant where he'd reserved a cosy table for two; presenting her with an exquisitely worked little gold and ruby brooch in the shape of a tiny fire over celebratory champagne cocktails—lest she forget how they met, he murmured with a quirk of a smile.

Willow grew to know Kitty and Jim well, discovering the couple were lovely people with hearts of gold. She was even able to distinguish each of the dogs by name after a while and appreciate their varying personalities. Although she was uncomfortably aware her love for Morgan was growing the more she got to know him, she couldn't seem to do anything about it, and he seemed determined she *did* get to know him. He shared more of his thoughts and emotions each time they met or spoke to each other on the phone during the week, but on the other hand his lovemaking was more restrained if anything, often leaving her frustrated and unhappy once they'd parted.

Monday to Friday became an eternity each week; she felt the longing for Morgan's presence like a physical pain. In spite of that she continued to ruthlessly dissect her feelings and was honest enough with herself to acknowledge part of her was relieved Morgan wasn't a for-ever type. It kept things strangely safe. He wasn't for her. And because of that she didn't have to decide whether she could trust him completely or if she was seeing the real man—all of him.

It was on the first weekend of November, a weekend which had ushered in the new month with a sudden drop in temperature and hard frosts, the glinting sparkle of spider webs and satisfying crunch of stiff white grass proclaiming it was going to be a cold winter, that things came to a head. In hindsight, Willow knew she had deliberately engineered the conversation which led to the row that followed. Seeing Morgan had become so bittersweet, her nerves were stretched as tight as a drum.

They were walking home as the sun set, the dogs gambolling in front of them in spite of having had a five-mile walk. Fleeting wisps of silver tinged the pink mother-of-pearl sky and the weather forecast had spoken of imminent snow. As they cut across a ploughed field towards the lane and home, the flash of a pheasant's iridescent plumage lit the sky as the bird rose just in front of the lead dog and flew into the air, squawking loudly in protest at being disturbed.

They stopped, and as Willow watched the pheasant disappear into a small copse some distance away, she murmured, 'Thank goodness it got away, I'd have hated for the dogs to kill it.'

Morgan nodded. 'So would I, but that's part of life in the country, I'm afraid.'

She glanced at him. 'And you would have been able to look at it like that? If the worst had happened?'

'You can't take instinct out of the dogs or the bird,' he said reasonably. 'The dogs will chase for the fun of it and the bird will flutter and excite them as it flies. They're being what they are and doing what they're programmed to do.'

'The age-old argument,' she muttered under her breath, but just loud enough for him to hear.

'I'm sorry?' He'd caught the sarcasm and as she met his gaze she saw the change in his eyes, the sudden wariness.

'The age-old argument the male population trot out to excuse all manner of things,' she said steadily, her heart thumping hard. 'You don't even realise you're doing it, do you?'

They had stopped walking and she raised her chin slightly as he studied her. 'I've never "trotted" anything out in my life, Willow. Nor do I hide behind excuses for my actions.'

'No?' She forced a disbelieving smile. 'I thought the nature thing all led up to most males' favourite theory, that it's unnatural for them to be monogamous? The old "bee gathering pollen from umpteen flowers" philosophy.'

A muscle twitched in Morgan's jaw. 'What's the matter?'

She tossed her head. 'Nothing's the matter.'

'I've obviously upset you in some way,' he said with infuriating calmness. 'I'm asking how.'

'I'm not upset. I'm just stating what is a well-known fact. Men in general are incapable of being faithful to one woman for the whole of their lives. I think it's something like eighty per cent or more will have an affair of some kind or other, even if their wife or long-term partner never finds out. And the most well-worn excuse is that they couldn't help it and it didn't mean anything, it was mere physical attraction.'

'Well, it looks as though I've learnt something more about that slimeball you married,' Morgan said coolly.

She drew in a gasp of shock. Whatever reaction she'd expected, it wasn't this. 'I don't know what you mean.'

'I think you do. Faithfulness wasn't one of his strong points.'

Willow stuffed her hands in the pockets of her coat and said overloudly, 'Every opinion I have doesn't relate back to Piers. I do actually have a mind of my own.'

The blue eyes glittered in the fading pearly light. 'Then I suggest you start using it.'

Her eyes widened. 'I beg your pardon?' she said angrily.

'You met and married one of life's emotional rejects and he put you through hell until you finished it. It was a mistake and we all make them. Deal with it and move on.'

Her life summed up Morgan-style. The anger was welcome; it provided the adrenalin needed to fight back. She glared at him. 'I don't need you to tell me how to conduct my life.'

'I think you do, because no one else can get near enough, can they? You've made sure of that. Even Beth watches what she says around you.'

'She does not!' She'd never been so furious. 'And what do you know about my relationship with my sister anyway? You've only met her once. Hardly a basis to judge anything by.'

The look on his face alerted her to the fact she'd inadvertently stumbled on something. She stared at him for a moment that seemed to stretch and swell. The dogs had gathered in a puzzled group about their legs, sensing all was not well.

'You've been talking to Beth,' she said flatly. 'Haven't you?'

He didn't deny it. 'I can talk to whomever I like.'

'You've been discussing me with my sister? How dare you, Morgan? How dare you contact Beth and talk to her about me?'

'As you have been so at pains to point out over the last little while, we're free, independent spirits, Willow,' he said with heavy sarcasm. 'That means I can do what I like, when I like and with whom. Or have I got that wrong?'

'I can't believe Beth would be so disloyal.'

'For crying out loud, will you listen to yourself?' Now he was glaring and she knew she'd pushed him beyond his limit. 'Your sister loves you very much and she's concerned about you—what's so terrible about that? Or is she now condemned to be placed with all the other untouchables that are kept on the perimeter of your life? When are you going to face the fact that you can't live as an island, Willow? Sooner or later you're going to have to let someone in.'

'That's rich, coming from you,' she tossed back with equal ferocity. 'Say as I say and not as I do. Is that your philosophy, Morgan? Because it stinks. If anyone is an island, you are, as you've made very plain from day one. No for ever for the great Morgan Wright, but if someone else dares to say the same thing it's wrong. Now what does that make you?'

'An emotional child, or at least I was,' he said, suddenly very calm. 'Until I met you. Then things changed. *I* changed. Not easily, I admit. I fought it every step of the way but I finally understood that I could no longer put my feelings and desires into neat, separate compartments any more. I don't want an affair with you, Willow. Until this very moment I hadn't realised how much I don't want that. I love you, not as a passing fancy or a temporary stopgap, but as my woman.'

'No, no, you don't.' She stepped backwards, stumbled but quickly righted herself as his arm reached out to steady her. As it fell back by his side, she said again, 'You don't. You said what you felt was physical attraction. You *said* that.'

'It is.' For a long moment he studied her face, his eyes searching hers. 'But that's only part of it.'

'No.' Panic had gripped her, she felt smothered, unable to breathe. She had done this, forced this thing that had been between them since the night he had stopped himself making love to her, out into the open. Now she couldn't pretend any more. And she had been pretending, fooling herself, lying. Instinctively she had known from that point on things were different and he hadn't been playing games. She wanted to believe in his sincerity now, to cast all doubts and fears aside and trust he was speaking the truth, that Morgan was as solid and genuine as Piers had been hollow and shallow, but it was too huge a step of faith to take. 'No, Morgan.'

'Yes,' he said. 'Yes. Whether you want to hear it or not, I love you, and it's about time I told you because something was threatening to give and it was my sanity.'

'You said we were carrying on as friends.'

'We were never friends.' There was brusqueness in his voice along with rawer emotion.

He was right. Friendship was far too tame a label. She tried to speak, failed, then cleared her throat. The air, the dogs, even the birds were still, everything—all nature—seemed suspended. She was conscious of bare-branched trees against the frosty sky and the delicate beauty hurt in view of what she was going to say.

Her throat had locked and she had to swallow hard before she could say, 'I'm sorry but I don't love you.'

She saw him flinch and for a moment the temptation to fling herself on him and take it back was strong, but what would be the outcome? Panic won and she stayed where she was, her gaze dropping from his. This had to end now, for good.

'If this was the movies or a love story I'd do the noble

thing and say it doesn't matter, that we can carry on as we are, that I've got enough love for the both of us,' Morgan said tersely. 'But it matters like hell and the last weeks have shown me my control can only be tested so far. I guess what I'm saying is that it has to be all or nothing with me, having come this close. Anything else is not an option any more.'

Struggling to match his control, Willow nodded. 'I—I can understand that.' It was like that for her too, if he did but know it. The trouble was, she didn't know if she could trust Morgan—any man—for the all. Raising her eyes, she looked into the ruggedly attractive face. He didn't deserve a nutcase like her, not after the childhood he'd endured and the knocks life had dished out. She was doing the right thing here.

Knowing she was going to howl like a banshee and make a total fool of herself, she said quickly, 'I'd better go. Th-thanks for everything. I'm sorry it's turned out this way.'

The blue eyes were boring into her soul. 'Willow—'

'It's for the best. Really, it's for the best.' She began to walk, knowing her movements were jerky but unable to do anything about it. She half expected him to walk with her and when he didn't, she waited for him to call her back. The call didn't come. She walked on but still it didn't come.

Willow reached the end of the field and stepped onto the small style that led into the lane. Then she was in the lane and walking swiftly, woodenly, aware of the cold air on her face and the smell of woodsmoke. Jim must have lit a bonfire, she thought vacantly. He often did on a Sunday afternoon.

By the time she reached the cottage the tears were streaming down her face and she fumbled with the key for what seemed like an age before the door opened. She all but fell across the threshold, pulling the door shut and then sinking down with her back against the wood as she sobbed and sobbed.

It was over. As she had wanted it to be. He thought she didn't love him and, Morgan being Morgan, that would be enough to keep him from contacting her again. No more hour-long phone calls, which had changed mediocre days into something wonderful; no more weekends filled with laughter and music and life; no more being able to watch his face as he talked and smiled; no more Morgan. What had she done? *What had she done?*

He had told her he loved her and she had flunked it big time, ruining any chance for them in the future. She couldn't have put the final seal on this relationship more effectively if she'd planned it for a lifetime, she thought sickly. She had lied to him and, in lying, sealed her fate.

Willow couldn't have said how long she sat there wallowing in misery, but by the time she dragged herself into the kitchen it was dark outside and beginning to snow. Fat, feathery flakes were falling in their millions from a laden sky. Willow wondered briefly if she was going to be able to get to work tomorrow, and then dismissed the thought just as quickly. What did work matter? What did anything matter? she asked herself wretchedly. If this was all there was, if life was going to continue to be as horrible as it had been the last few years, she might as well hibernate in the cottage and become a recluse.

After making herself a mug of hot chocolate she put a match to the fire and curled up on the sofa, staring unseeing into the burgeoning flames. Morgan said he loved her, but how could she know he wouldn't change once they were together? She didn't let herself consider marriage; togetherness was too frightening as it was. And he hadn't mentioned marriage anyway.

Piers had been the perfect boyfriend before they'd got wed: charming, amusing, loving, attentive. He hadn't put a foot wrong and she'd thought she was the luckiest girl in the world. And then they'd tied the knot and even on honeymoon he'd begun to show his true colours. How could anyone ever really know anyone else?

'They can't,' she whispered into her mug of hot chocolate, cupping her hands round its warmth. They can't, that's the truth of it. Some things had to be taken on trust and she was all out of that commodity. She couldn't, she just couldn't, take the risk.

Wiping her eyes with the back of her hand, she told herself to get a grip. She had a nice job, her own home and she was in good health. Furthermore, she had plenty of friends and was as free as a bird to do what she pleased. She was so lucky.

It didn't help. It should have, but it didn't.

After another hour or so of fruitless soul-searching she resolutely switched on the TV. The weather girl was happily warning of severe snowstorms causing major traffic problems, her hands waving like an air hostess as she pointed out the worst-hit areas. It looked worse directly where Willow lived.

Great, Willow thought. Still, she was warm and snug and had plenty of food. Even if she was kept home for a day or two it wouldn't matter. She sat gazing at the TV screen wondering if Morgan would come round to see if she was all right if they got snowed in. He might, she thought, her heart thudding, before picturing the look on his face when she'd said she didn't love him. Of course he wouldn't come. Why would he? Silly to expect it. He might go as far as sending Jim but he wouldn't come himself. Not now. He'd stay away because he thought she wanted him to.

After another bout of crying she watched an inane comedy, which even the studio audience didn't seem to find funny judging by the forced laughter, and then made herself more hot chocolate. She had just swallowed two headache pills when her mobile phone rang, causing her heart to jump into her throat.

Her hands trembling, she looked at the number and could have cried again but this time with disappointment. Beth's mobile. Likely her sister and Peter were out somewhere and checking she was safely at home in view of the weather. She was still faintly annoyed that Beth and Morgan had been having private conversations she'd known nothing about, and her voice was stiff when she said, 'Hallo, Beth?'

'It's me, Peter.'

She knew immediately something was badly wrong; she'd never heard stolid, reliable Peter's voice shake before.

'Beth's had a fall. I'm ringing on her phone because when the ambulance came I forgot mine but Beth's was in her handbag.'

Blow whose phone he was using. 'Where are you? What's happened?' she said urgently. 'Is Beth badly hurt?'

'We're at the hospital. Beth fell down the cellar steps earlier. Why the hell she went down there without telling me I don't know; apparently she wanted to sort the last of the packing cases we stored down there when we moved.

It had something in she wanted for the baby's room. The first I knew I heard her scream—' His voice broke, then he went on, 'She landed awkwardly, Willow. They—they think the baby's coming.'

A month early. Endeavouring to keep the alarm out of her voice, she said quickly, 'It might be a false labour, Peter. A reaction to the fall. Things might calm down. They often do.'

'No, we thought that at first but now they're pretty sure it's coming. Her waters have broken and everything.'

'Three or four weeks early is nothing these days,' she said reassuringly, 'and babies are tougher than you think. It'll be fine, I know it will. Beth's healthy so don't worry.'

'She's asking for you. Is there any chance of you coming to the hospital tonight? She…she needs you with her, Willow.'

She didn't have to think about it. 'Absolutely. I'll be there as soon as I can. I'll leave straight away.'

'Drive carefully though, the roads are already getting pretty bad,' Peter said worriedly. 'When you get here, go to the maternity reception and they'll direct you. OK? I'll tell them you're coming and explain so there won't be any problems.'

'That's fine. Now get back to Beth and hold her hand, and don't forget to give her my love and tell her I'm on my way.'

'Thanks, Willow.' His voice was husky. 'I appreciate it.'

She stared at the phone for a stunned moment once the call had finished, and then leapt into action. Five minutes later she was dressed in warmer clothes, the fire was banked down and the guard was in place, and everything was off that needed to be off.

When she opened the front door and the force of the wind

threatened to tear it out of her fingers, she realised how bad the storm had become. Already the snow was inches thick and it showed no signs of abating, just the opposite.

Pulling her hat more firmly over her ears, she staggered to the car, wondering if she was going to be able to get out of the lane, let alone all the way to the hospital. In the event she needn't have worried. The engine was as dead as a dodo.

She tried everything, including crying, praying and finally stamping her feet and screaming like a two-year-old. It was after this she accepted she was going nowhere in this car tonight. She would have to phone for a taxi. It was going to cost a small fortune but it wasn't the time to count the cost. Beth needed her. Whatever it took, she was going to get to that hospital. 'Hold on, Beth,' she prayed. 'I'm coming.'

CHAPTER TWELVE

MORGAN sat staring down at the papers on his desk. He'd been sitting in the same position for a while, his mind replaying for the umpteenth time the whole disastrous last conversation with Willow. In fact ever since he'd got home and immediately gone to his study, telling Kitty he had some urgent financial reports to look through, he'd been dissecting every word, every gesture, every glance they'd exchanged. It had been a relief when Kitty and Jim had turned in early due to the weather, and he'd had the house to himself. He appreciated Kitty's motherly concern for his welfare, but there was the odd occasion when he was very thankful their flat was situated over the garages and separate from the main house, and this was one of them. He couldn't stand her fussing tonight.

He scowled at the inoffensive papers. He didn't know how Kitty knew he'd fed most of his supper to the dogs, but she'd looked at the empty plate and then at him and asked him point blank if he and Willow had had an argument. He'd snapped at her then, something he felt guilty about now.

Moving restlessly, he rose to his feet and went to stand

by the fire, his back to the flames. She was a good woman, Kitty. Gentle, kind. If he'd been placed with someone like her as a boy, his childhood would have been different.

Don't start feeling sorry for yourself, for crying out loud. Self-contempt brought him straightening his shoulders before he bent to pick up another log to throw on the fire.

He'd been lucky. Overall, he'd been very lucky to get to where he was now. He'd worked hard, of course, but then so did lots of folk who never got the break he'd got. One of his friends had said he'd got the Midas touch where business was concerned, and maybe he had. It had enabled him to rise in the world, to become more wealthy and successful than he had ever dreamed of in his youth, and he had dreamed plenty.

Morgan smiled bitterly. He'd vowed every day of his childhood and teenage years that he would make something of himself, if only to show the relatives who had treated him so shamefully that he'd had the last laugh. And one by one they'd come sniffing around once he'd made his first million or two, hands held out. It had given him great satisfaction to tell them exactly where they could go.

Yes, until a few weeks ago he'd been satisfied he had everything a man could possibly wish for in life. *Until Willow.* He'd really thought he was getting somewhere with her the last little while, though; there had been something different about her since that night when he had surprised her by walking away.

He should have taken her and be damned, he told himself savagely in the next moment, spinning on his heel so sharply that the dogs—scattered about the floor—rose as one to their feet with low barks. If he had taken her that night she would probably have been in his arms right now. But he had wanted more than the pleasure of her company in bed; he still did, more fool him. He had slept with many women in his time but until Willow he hadn't wanted to make love with one, and there was a difference. Oh, yes, there was a difference.

'Enough,' he muttered as he crossed the hall. He was going to have a drink. In fact more than one. A lot more. Enough so that when he closed his eyes tonight he would sleep without thinking or dreaming. Oblivion would be sweet tonight.

The sound of the front door bell stopped him in his tracks and sent the dogs charging to perform their canine duty of repelling invaders. Morgan frowned. Who the dickens was that on a night like this? Someone who'd broken down possibly, but he had never felt less like playing the good Samaritan in his life. He could do nothing less than answer the door, though.

One sharp word of command brought the pack of dogs slinking behind him, ears pricked and eyes narrowed, as he opened the door.

'I'm so sorry, Morgan.' She was speaking before he'd even got the door properly open. 'I would never have bothered you normally but Beth's in the hospital and I have to get there and my car won't start and the taxi cabs are refusing to turn out—'

'Hey, hey, hey.' He interrupted the frantic gabble by reaching out and drawing the snow-covered figure into the warmth of the house. 'Slowly now. From the beginning, Willow.'

'Peter phoned me. Beth's had a fall and the baby's

coming early and she wants me there. I promised, Morgan, but my car won't start and no taxis are running because of the weather. I didn't know what to do…'

'Yes, you did,' he said quietly. 'You came to me and I'll sort it. The snow won't bother the Range-Rover. We'll get through. I'll get my things. Relax, it'll be all right.'

They stopped outside the garage block and Morgan explained to Jim what was happening, then they were on the road and on their way. Willow had always thought that snow was pretty, transforming even the dullest landscape into a winter wonderland. Tonight she hated it. It was a relentless enemy and unforgiving.

In spite of the powerful four by four's ability to tackle the most atrocious weather conditions, she could see Morgan was having his work cut out to keep the vehicle moving steadily forward. She sat in an agony of impatience as they passed abandoned cars every few miles; the snow was forming into great drifts in places and the roads were swiftly becoming impassable. They didn't speak; she knew Morgan needed every ounce of concentration if they were going to reach the hospital safely, but she wouldn't have known what to say anyway. She had turned up on his doorstep needing his help—yet again—and even after all that had happened that afternoon he hadn't hesitated or made her feel bad. His response had been immediate and unconditional. He was a man in a million.

She glanced at him under her eyelashes. He was hunched over the wheel, peering into the road ahead as the windscreen wipers laboured under their burden of snow, every muscle and sinew focused on the job in hand. She was cold, tired, worried and scared to death, but there was no one in the world she'd rather be with in this situation than Morgan. Ninety-nine out of a hundred men wouldn't have dreamt of turning out on a night like this for a nightmare journey, certainly not for a woman who had thrown their love back in their face only hours earlier. Piers wouldn't have put his nose out of the door for his own sister, let alone hers. She couldn't compare Morgan to Piers, or any other man if it came to it. Morgan was Morgan, a one-off. Unique. And he loved her. As she did him.

The wind was whipping the car and great swirls of snow were blasting the windows, but for the first time since she had met Morgan the storm within Willow was quietened. Any regrets she felt about the past would be nothing to what she'd feel if she lost Morgan through her own cowardice. She hadn't liked his straight talking earlier, but he was right—it was time to move on. Every word he'd said to her was true.

The Range-Rover crawled the last few miles to the hospital and they were within sight of the building when the snow finally won the battle. Two cars had slewed across the road thereby blocking it completely, and turning round wasn't an option.

'Looks like the last leg will have to be on foot.' Morgan cut the engine as he spoke, stretching his arms above his head for a moment. 'Hold on to me and we'll get there, OK?'

He had just encapsulated her thoughts for the future more neatly than he'd ever know. Quietly, she said, 'I'm sorry I dragged you out on a night like this. You seem forever destined to rescue me from one disaster or another.'

'Beth falling down the cellar steps can hardly be laid at your door.' He smiled. 'Nor the blizzard.'

She smiled back. 'Thank you,' she said softly.

A shadow passed over his face but it had gone so swiftly she thought she had imagined it. Words hovered on her lips, explanations, excuses, but then she nearly jumped out of her skin as someone tapped Morgan's window.

The police officer informed them the road ahead was impassable, as if they didn't know. 'This is not a night to be out, sir,' he added, 'and all the signs are the storm's getting worse. Have you far to go?'

Willow chimed in. 'My sister's expecting a baby and we're trying to reach the hospital. It's not far from here.'

The policeman nodded. 'You'll do that all right, but I suggest you think about staying there the night. Come morning things will be easier but any journey tonight is foolhardy. People don't realise how treacherous these sort of conditions can be. Stay in the hospital and keep warm.'

'We'll do just that, Officer,' Morgan said appeasingly.

Once the policeman had trudged off, looking more like Frosty the Snowman than anything else, Willow said again, 'I *am* sorry to have put you in this position, Morgan. Will the Range-Rover be OK to leave here until morning?'

'It'll be fine.' His tone was dismissive, even curt.

Again she told herself to *say* something but the moment—and her courage—was gone.

She watched as Morgan walked round and opened her door, helping her down into the snow, which immediately rode over the old boots she'd pulled on before leaving the cottage. The snow was blinding and she was glad of Morgan's arm around her once they began walking. Far from being the enchantingly feathery stuff of fairy tales, this snow was vicious. It stung the eyes and lashed the skin, making the several hundred yards to the hospital an ordeal. She'd never experienced snow like this.

When they reached the automatic doors leading into the maternity section of the hospital, the warmth hit them as they walked in. Willow made herself known at Reception as Peter had instructed, and the efficient hospital machine kicked in. Within a few minutes a bright, cheery little blonde nurse was standing in front of them. She explained Willow needed to be fitted with a hospital gown before she joined her sister in the delivery room, and Morgan could wait in a special area designed for that purpose close to the room where Beth and Peter were.

Willow wondered if the girl's fluttering eyelashes and bold smile had registered on Morgan, but gratifyingly she rather thought not. He'd been equally oblivious to other women's interested glances in the past too, although she'd found them irritating to say the least.

She forgot about the nurse when she walked into Beth's room, knowing she'd never forget the look on her sister's face when Beth saw her. She spent the next little while between contractions assuring Beth that *of course* the baby was fine and *lots* came early, and were happy and healthy; praying inwardly all the time it was true. Beth would never forgive herself if things went wrong.

As time went on the contractions got stronger and the minutes between them less, but Beth wouldn't hear of her leaving. It was another three hours before the baby was born. It was a boy and he was a good weight, his lusty lungs proclaiming all was well as he bellowed his way into the world.

Willow was misty-eyed and Peter was crying unashamedly, but Beth was radiant as the nurse put the baby into her arms. 'This is David Peter,' she said, glancing at Willow who nodded her understanding. David had been their father's name. As Beth glanced towards the window, she seemed to realise it was snowing for the first time. 'How did you get here?' she asked. 'You didn't drive in this, did you?'

Willow smiled at her sister. 'I came courtesy of Morgan's white horse, although it was the four by four this time, not the Harley.'

It was totally against hospital rules, the nurse murmured a little while later after she had been to see the sister, but what with the storm and all everything was topsy-turvy tonight. If Mr Wright only stayed for a minute or two the sister would turn a blind eye this once. Beth nodded and assured the nurse sixty seconds would do it. 'Go and fetch him,' she said to Willow after the nurse had left. 'I want him to feel included in this; but for him you wouldn't have got here tonight.'

It was more than that and they both knew it. Willow hugged her sister. 'I love you,' she whispered softly, marvelling at how her world—which had seemed so disastrously out of kilter when she had stumbled through the snow to Morgan's house earlier—was righting itself. If she had the courage of her convictions, that was.

The waiting room was in semi-darkness when she reached it, the subdued lighting presumably so that its occupants could grab a little sleep if they needed it. It had worked with Morgan anyway.

Willow tiptoed in. How he had managed to fall asleep on one of the so-called 'comfy' chairs in the waiting room she didn't know. The wooden arms and plastic stretched tight over lumpy stuffing would have kept a sleeping-sickness sufferer awake. But he was dead to the world, his long legs stretched out at an impossible angle and his head draped over the back of the chair.

It was the first time she had been able to study his face without fear of those piercing eyes arresting her. He looked exhausted. Her gaze stroked over the tough masculine features. But younger, more susceptible than when he was awake. How couldn't she have seen his vulnerability before?

Because she had been too hung up on the past to look beyond herself and her own feelings.

The truth was uncomfortable but then it often was. When he had spoken of his childhood and youth she hadn't pressed him for details, telling herself it was probably too painful for him to share. But that had been an excuse. She had been frightened of learning anything that would endear him further to her. The experiences he had gone through as a boy had shaped him into the complicated and enigmatic man he was today, that was for sure, but he had a capacity for love and tenderness she couldn't ignore any longer. She couldn't let him slip through her fingers.

She had to tell him how she felt and trust she hadn't ruined everything. She nodded to the thought, ignoring the panic that accompanied it. She owed him that at least.

Willow knelt down beside the chair, drinking in the sight and scent of him. He'd discarded the thick leather jacket he'd worn in the car and his sweater did little to disguise the width of his chest and muscled strength of his shoulders. His hair had got damp as they'd walked and now it curled slightly over his forehead, accentuating the suggestion of boyishness. He was a man of contradictions, impossible to fathom.

'Morgan?' She touched his arm gently, her voice little more than a whisper. 'Morgan, wake up. It's me, Willow.'

His eyelids flickered and opened slowly but he didn't move. His voice so low she could barely make out the words, he murmured, 'I was dreaming of you.'

'A good dream?' she whispered, loving him so much it hurt.

His eyes seemed bluer than she'd ever seen them before and the faint lines radiating from their corners crinkled as he smiled. 'X-rated.'

It was probably unfair to take advantage of him when he was still half asleep, but it was now or never. 'I lied to you this afternoon,' she said softly. 'I do love you. I love you like I never thought it was possible to love anyone and I've known it for a while. Can—can you forgive me?'

He didn't move, not a muscle. For what seemed an endless moment he stared at her, his face unreadable.

Willow stared back, equally immobile, holding her breath as her heart thudded so hard she was sure he must be able to hear it. Let it be all right, she prayed. Please let it be all right.

And then, as though lit from within, the hard rugged features melted in a smile that was beautiful. He opened his arms as he sat up in the chair and she scrambled into them, tilting her head back for his kiss, her mouth as hungry as his.

'I love you, I do, I do,' she murmured feverishly between kisses. 'And I'm so sorry I hurt you. I hated myself this afternoon but I was so scared, Morgan. I still am scared. I can't help it.'

'And you think I'm not?' he murmured against her lips.

'Sweetheart, this frightens me to the core. My life was all mapped out and I was doing very nicely until you came along and blew me out of the water.'

'Did I?'

'Did you what?'

'Blow you out of the water.'

'Oh, baby, did you ever.'

They kissed again, straining together in an agony of need and murmuring incoherent words of love until a sound in the corridor outside brought them back to earth. Raising his head reluctantly, Morgan said softly, 'Beth? How is she?'

'She's fine, the baby too. They've got a little boy and you're allowed to see him, just for a minute. You're not supposed to but Beth got special permission.'

'Special permission, eh?' He kissed her nose, his voice teasing to disguise the gratification he felt at being included. 'This is pure you, you know,' he said tenderly, 'finally telling me you love me in a hospital waiting room with a blizzard outside and your sister just having given birth. It should have been over an intimate meal for two with wine and candles and guitars throbbing in the background.'

Willow giggled. 'You told me you loved me in the middle of a freezing cold ploughed field when we were having a row,' she reminded him.

'Oh, boy, do we have a lot to make up for…' He took her face in his big hands, smiling shakily as he murmured, 'But in for a penny, in for a pound. This should be done with music and a ring to hand and me on one knee but I have to know. Will you marry me? Will you be my wife, to have and to hold for ever?'

Somewhere outside their room a bell was being rung impatiently; someone was clattering along with what sounded like a trolley in the corridor and the odd baby or two were crying in the background. The smell of antiseptic was strong along with that faint odour peculiar to all hospitals, which was impossible to pin down. Willow thought she had never been in such a perfect place. 'Yes,' she said, taking his lips in a kiss that was fierce. 'Yes, yes, yes.'

Beth's squeal of delight brought the nurse running when Willow gave her sister the news after she and Morgan had held David Peter for a moment or two. For such a big man, Morgan had held the tiny infant with a tender delicacy that had wrenched her heart. She'd had a vision of the future, of Morgan cradling their own baby with the same sweet gentleness, and it had reduced her to tears. Not that it mattered. Tears and smiles and laughter were flowing with abandon and had infected everyone with the same weakness.

By the time she and Morgan returned to the waiting room Willow felt dizzy with happiness. That and tiredness. It was now gone three in the morning. She felt ridiculously hungry too but the hospital restaurant and café didn't open for breakfast for another five hours. Morgan found a snack machine and returned with crisps, chocolate bars and two paper cups holding a murky brown liquid that purported to be hot chocolate.

She sat on Morgan's lap and they fed each other the food between kisses, cocooned in a couple of blankets the nurse had kindly brought them. They didn't talk about the past or the future; that could come later. They had time now, for everything. But tonight only the present mattered; being in each other's arms, able to kiss and touch and breathe the other's warmth.

If this wasn't heaven, it was close enough, Willow thought as she snuggled against his chest and shut her eyes. Thank goodness for Beth wanting her tonight, thank goodness for the snow and her car not starting and the fact it was the weekend and Morgan had been home; thank goodness that against all the odds she had found the one man who could release her from the past and make her life complete.

She settled herself more comfortably within the circle of Morgan's arms and within moments she was asleep, a half-smile on her lips and her body curled trustingly into his.

CHAPTER THIRTEEN

THEY got married on Christmas Eve at the little parish church in the village. How Morgan managed to pull everything together so quickly, Willow didn't know. It wasn't just the paperwork and legal stuff, but persuading the vicar to fit in the marriage service between the three carol concerts the church was holding that day that amazed her. She suspected a hefty donation towards the church-roof fund might have had something to do with it. Certainly the vicar seemed happy enough.

Willow wore a mermaid-style dress in pale gold guipure lace with a fake-fur-lined matching cloak and hood, and carried a Christmas bouquet. Peter was giving her away and as they reached the church and heard the organ music as they stood outside she gripped his arm tightly. 'Oh, Peter.'

'Everything's going to be fine,' he reassured her softly, 'and you look beautiful. You'll take his breath away.'

She smiled at him tremulously. She had no doubts about what she was doing but she suddenly felt so emotional as she looked at the arch of Christmas garlands hung round the church door. The December day was bitterly cold but sparkling with sunshine and the winter sky was as blue as

Morgan's eyes. She hoped her parents knew how happy she was, how happy both she and Beth were. She hoped they knew they had their first grandchild, and that she was thinking of them on this special day. She hoped…oh, lots of things.

'Ready?' Peter smiled down at her and she nodded. As they stepped into the church's tiny inner porch the music changed, announcing her arrival, and just for a second she remembered that other wedding. She'd worn a full meringue-style dress in white satin with a long veil that day and they'd had nearly three hundred guests to the reception. Piers had insisted on a very formal and grand affair and her five bridesmaids and two flower girls had been schooled by him—as had she—not to put a foot wrong. She'd felt nervous and tense all day and the dress had been too tight, the speeches too long and she'd developed a blinding headache before the day was half through. Piers, on the other hand, had been in his element.

This was so different. Their seventy guests were all close friends and family and Kitty had put on a magnificent spread at home. This was an impromptu wedding filled with love.

Slowly and gracefully she began to walk down the aisle towards the tall dark man standing beside Jim at the front of the church. Morgan turned to watch her and the blue eyes were glittering with tears as she reached him. With no respect of etiquette he bent and kissed her as he took her cold little hand in his, and immediately his warmth and love surrounded her. She smiled up at him, all her adoration in her eyes.

He kept tight hold of her hand as the minister began the service, and when the time came to say their vows his voice was strong and clear for all to hear. By then the brief poignant sadness outside the church had gone and she was glowing with happiness. She was with Morgan. Where she belonged. And she knew that, for better or worse, in sickness and in health, for richer or poorer, until death did them part, they would be there for each other, strong in their love.

When the vicar beamingly declared them man and wife Morgan lifted her off her feet and swung her round to cheers from the congregation, kissing her soundly as she clung to him, her cheeks rosy pink and her eyes shining. Beth and Kitty cried along with the rest of the women in the church, and there was even the odd male guest who had a surreptitious dab at his eyes, but Willow and Morgan were smiling as they walked down the aisle together looking radiant. Which made Beth cry still more.

A friend of Morgan's who was also a professional photographer took relaxed, natural pictures throughout the afternoon and even little David Peter beamed toothlessly into the camera. The food was delicious, the champagne flowed and everyone got a little tiddly by evening when the dancing started in the huge, heated marquee in the garden, which was decorated with Christmas garlands.

Willow felt she was floating in a dream when she and Morgan had the first dance, their guests gathered in a smiling circle around them. It had been the perfect day. She glanced at the rose-gold wedding band nestling next to the diamond engagement ring Morgan had bought her the day after he'd proposed. Her hand was resting on his shoulder and he caught her glance, his voice deep and husky when he said, 'It's there for life, sweetheart.'

'I know.' She smiled up at her brand-new husband, thinking he was the most handsome, sexy, delicious man in the world as he whirled her round the dance floor.

'Don't look at me like that,' he whispered in her ear, his warm breath tickling her cheek, 'or we won't finish this dance, let alone the rest of the evening, before I take you upstairs and rip that dress off.'

'It cost a fortune,' she protested laughingly. 'You have to undo all the little buttons down the back.'

He groaned. 'What's wrong with a good old-fashioned zip?'

'Morgan, this is a designer wedding dress,' she said with mock severity.

'Exactly.' He grinned down at her. 'And the designer should have known better.'

She touched his face with her fingertips. He had insisted they would wait until their wedding night—hence the swift arrangements and bribe to the vicar—because he wanted it to be special with her, different from all those other women he had bedded so casually. She respected him for that and understood his reasoning, but she had seen what his restraint had cost him over the last weeks. But now the time for restraint was over and she wanted him every little bit as much as he wanted her. Beneath the guipure lace she was wearing a low-cut sexy bra, positively indecent see-through briefs and stockings, her pièce de résistance a naughty little garter.

Beth's eyes had nearly popped out of her head when she'd helped her dress in her wedding finery that morning. 'Willow!' her sister had shrieked. 'You dark horse, you.'

Her cheeks scarlet, Willow had muttered, 'What is it with

you and horses, Beth? And I don't usually go for this sort of underwear,' she'd added as Beth had laboured over the host of tiny buttons at the back of the gown. 'But I wanted to surprise him. To let him know how much I want him.'

'You will. Oh, you will.'

The memory of that conversation brought her mouth turning upwards now, and as the dance finished and they were joined by other couples Morgan murmured, 'What is it?'

Feeling deliciously like a wanton hussy, she murmured back, 'I've got a surprise for you later.' She might not be able to match those other women he'd known in expertise or a knowledge of all the little tricks a woman could use to please a man of the world like Morgan, but she had something none of them had had. His love.

The first guests began to leave about eleven, and by midnight they waved the last straggler off. Kitty and Jim had retired to their flat above the garages long ago and Kitty had promised she wouldn't disturb them until she called them for Christmas Day lunch at one o'clock the next afternoon. The day after that they were flying to Hawaii for a month's honeymoon. Morgan had booked a little villa right on the beach.

They stood wrapped in each other's arms on the doorstep as the lights of the car faded down the drive. A million stars twinkled in a clear velvet sky and the frost glittered like diamond dust on the ground, thick and white. The dogs had gone out as they'd seen their guests off and now filed past them into the warmth of the house, sensing it was their bedtime at last. They'd accepted her presence in Morgan's life completely.

Morgan grinned at her. 'We've been keeping them up. I think they were ready for bed long before this.'

She turned in his arms, kissing him hungrily. 'Them and me both,' she murmured. 'I didn't think the last few would ever go.'

With a groan of longing he pulled her into him and then lifted her off her feet, carrying her over the threshold for the second time that day. Kicking the door shut behind him, he held her high against his chest as he kissed her, devouring her mouth as she yielded to his maleness, her body boneless and fluid against his. She was trembling but not with fright, and as his mouth crushed hers possessively she strained against him, wanting more, passionate and willing for all the love he had to give.

By the time they reached the bedroom they were both breathing raggedly, their faces flushed. From somewhere Morgan found the strength to slow down. This had to be so right for her after all she had been through and he didn't want to rush it. They had a thousand tomorrows and he would make sure they were all filled with happiness and fulfilment but tonight—tonight was precious, a night apart. Tonight she became his wife.

An ice-bucket with a bottle of the best champagne and two flutes, along with a huge bowl of hothouse strawberries, was standing on a small table close to the bed. He made himself walk across and pour two glasses after he had set her down on her feet, returning immediately and placing one glass in her fingers before he said, 'To us, Mrs Wright.'

She smiled up at him and touched his cheek with her palm. 'To us, Mr Wright. And you are right for me, so right.'

They drank deeply before he set the glasses down and took her in his arms again, covering her face with kisses before he turned her round and began to undo the tiny buttons, kissing and nuzzling her shoulders and the nape of her neck as he did so. He edged the dress apart, caressing the silky skin of her back, before continuing with the myriad buttons, swearing softly once or twice when a particular button resisted his efforts and making her giggle.

'Of all the dresses in all the world…'

'I wanted to look beautiful for you,' she murmured softly.

'Believe me, my darling, you don't need clothes for that.'

When the final button gave up the fight he turned her round to face him and as he did so she let the dress fall to the floor. The look of wonder on his face was all she could have wished for. 'My surprise,' she whispered, suddenly overcome with shyness at the expression on his face. 'Happy wedding day.'

'You're more beautiful than words can say,' he breathed against her skin, his hands cupping her breasts as his mouth explored her curves. He peeled off her bra and then her stockings, taking his time, using his hands and mouth with exquisitely controlled sensuality as he knelt before her. When he removed the scrap of material that was her panties, followed lastly by the garter, she tugged at his hair.

'My turn,' she murmured plaintively.

He smiled, rising to his feet and standing before her as she undressed him. Now it was she who stroked and tasted the contours of his body, the hard muscles that shivered under her fingers and the roughness of his body hair exciting her as she teased him. By the time he was naked he was hugely aroused.

He lifted her up and carried her over to the bed, placing her on the black satin sheets and lying down beside her. She had half expected that their first time would be a quick and lusty coupling born of the desire he had kept a rein on for so long, but Morgan spent a long time showing her differently. He kissed and tasted and caressed every inch of her until she was mindless beneath him and begging for the release only he could give. And still he continued to please her.

She had never dreamt her body was capable of what it was feeling, that it was possible for pleasure to reach such a pitch that it was unbearable in its intensity. He introduced her to things she'd had no idea of, things that would have made her blush in the cold light of day but which were so right in the warm womb of their room. And all the time he whispered words of love and passion, taking care not to hurt her, her pleasure his only focus.

She was sleek and wet when finally he nudged her thighs apart and entered her, moving slowly, carefully at first, conscious it had been a while for her and she would be tight. She was tight, but his ministrations had prepared her body to receive its satin-hard invader.

He filled her completely, the sensation extremely satisfying, and as he began to move with gentle thrusts to build her pleasure small rhythmic contractions began to grow deep inside, sending shivers throughout her body. And still he took his time, building passion until she no longer recognised who she was. Until she merged into him and he into her.

She knew the moment he surrendered to his own desire; suddenly he was moving faster and deeper, his voice hoarse as he groaned her name with each thrust of his body. They reached their culmination together, spiralling off into a world of colour and light and sensation that held no past and no future, just the glorious present. Morgan gave a single raw cry of fierce gratification, collapsing on top of her seconds later as he turned and drew her against him, still joined. They were both gasping for breath but slowly the frantic pounding of their hearts quietened and their eyes opened.

It was only then Willow was able to speak, her voice dazed as she whispered, 'I never knew…'

It was ample reward for his patience and restraint and he smiled, smoothing her hair back before kissing her forehead. 'You're amazing,' he murmured softly, kissing her again.

'It—it was good for you?'

He recognised the thread of doubt, the need for reassurance, and love for her made his voice husky when he said, 'It was better than good, my love. I fell off the edge of the world.'

Her voice carried laughter in it now when she said, 'That good, eh?' as she tangled her fingers in the soft hair of his chest.

He stroked her back, her waist. 'You're all I could ever have hoped for, all I could have dreamed of, and I will love you till the day I die and beyond. I would give my life for you and consider it well lost, and I will never betray your trust in me by thought or word or deed.'

She touched her fingers to his mouth, her face blazing with love. 'I know,' she said, and she did. 'Because I feel the same.' She snuggled deeper into him, feeling his body respond instantly. 'Morgan,' she whispered, 'do you realise we might have made a baby?'

His voice held amusement when he said, 'I have to admit that wasn't high on my list of priorities for tonight, but, yes, we agreed we wouldn't use precautions so I suppose it's possible from now on.'

'But we might not have done,' she said after a moment.

'No, we might not.'

She lifted her eyes to his and they were glinting with laughter. 'So we could always increase the odds, couldn't we?' She twisted her hips and heard his sharp intake of breath as she rubbed against him.

'Absolutely.'

They made love twice more before finally falling asleep in each other's arms when it was light and church bells were celebrating the birth of the Saviour. Willow's last lucid thought was that from now on she would spend her nights in this man's arms and wake up in the morning to the sound of his breathing and the promise of making love with him and feeling his arms holding her. Her body felt sensuously satisfied, her mind was at peace and she wanted to stay like this for ever. She slept.

EPILOGUE

WILLOW didn't get her wedding-night baby, but exactly twelve months to the day they married, on a snowy Christmas Eve, their twin daughters made their appearance into the world.

Willow and Morgan hadn't planned on a home birth—with it being twins and a first pregnancy they'd been advised a hospital confinement would be advisable—but the speed of the labour took everyone, including Willow, by surprise. Morgan ended up delivering the babies with Beth's help as Beth, Peter and little David had been spending the day with them.

By the time the midwife reached the house after Morgan's frantic telephone call, it was all over. Holly and Ivy were tucked up in bed with their mother having their first feed, the strains of the carol that featured their names filtering up from the kitchen below where an ecstatic Kitty was making everyone a cup of tea.

'Goodness me.' The midwife's face was a picture as she stood surveying the happy scene. 'And you say you only had your first pain a couple of hours ago? This isn't how it's normally done, believe me.'

'Oh, I do,' Beth said in heartfelt tones.

Morgan, who was sitting on the edge of the bed with his arm round Willow and one hand stroking the downy head of one of his daughters, smiled. 'We've something of a reputation for doing things our own way,' he murmured lazily. 'Isn't that right, sweetheart?'

Willow smiled back. He might have reverted to the cool, slightly laconic Morgan he liked to show the world, but a little while ago he'd been beside himself. It had certainly been a baptism of fire into parenthood. She'd had mild backache for the last twenty-four hours and had been slightly uncomfortable after lunch, but none of them had dreamed she was in labour. And now they had two daughters. She glanced down at the babies nestled against her and then looked at Morgan. The blue eyes were waiting for her and their expression touched her to the core.

Sometimes in the night he would reach for her to hold her close, not necessarily to make love but just to enfold her into him and feel her breathing and warm against him. She knew she was his world and every day she thanked God for what they had. And now they were parents and their love, like the amoeba, would metamorphose to embrace their family. And they had plans for the future, plans as yet they hadn't shared with anyone else.

This house was so big and the grounds were wonderful, and although they wanted another child of their own in the future they had discussed adopting a couple—perhaps even more—of older children who had been placed in social care through no fault of their own. Children with health problems maybe, or who were disabled in some way—children no one else wanted to adopt because it might be too much of a headache.

Morgan remembered so well how he had wanted a family and a home of his own when he had been growing up, how desperately he had tried to make his relatives love and keep him, how he had felt when eventually he had been moved on to the next place. And eventually he had stopped hoping or believing that anyone would ever want him, hiding behind toughness and autonomy and taking the world by the throat.

They had talked through the painful memories together, slowly bringing into the light the recollection of cold dark nights when a little boy had been curled up in a strange bed yet again, or standing apart from the family he happened to be with watching other children receiving gifts or sweets or a hug, and knowing there was none for him.

Their family would *be* a family, they were united on this, and their children would be loved and cared for regardless of whether they were theirs biologically or not. Kitty and Jim would be perfect grandparents and right on tap to help too, because they didn't fool themselves things would always be easy or plain sailing. Not where damaged little people were concerned. But love could move mountains and break down the most carefully constructed barricades; it had smashed those around Morgan's heart, hadn't it? Her own too.

The babies had stopped suckling, and as Beth helped the midwife check them over in their little individual Moses baskets Willow reached up and touched Morgan's cheek. 'I love you so much,' she whispered. 'And I'm so blissfully happy.'

He brought her fingers to his lips, kissing each one. 'I love you too. Thank you for our beautiful daughters.'

'Pretty personalised Christmas gift, don't you think?'

He smiled quizzically. 'What are you going to do for next year? How on earth are you going to top this?'

She dimpled up at him, and as Kitty walked in with a tray whispered, 'I'll think of something.'

'Now that, my love, I don't doubt…'

HARLEQUIN® Presents®

Coming Next Month

in **Harlequin Presents®.** Available August 31, 2010.

#2939 MARRIAGE: TO CLAIM HIS TWINS
Penny Jordan
Needed: The World's Most Eligible Billionaires

#2940 KAT AND THE DARE-DEVIL SPANIARD
Sharon Kendrick
The Balfour Brides

#2941 THE ANDREOU MARRIAGE ARRANGEMENT
Helen Bianchin

#2942 THE BILLIONAIRE'S HOUSEKEEPER MISTRESS
Emma Darcy
At His Service

#2943 ONE NIGHT...NINE-MONTH SCANDAL
Sarah Morgan

#2944 THE VIRGIN'S PROPOSITION
Anne McAllister

Coming Next Month

in **Harlequin Presents® EXTRA.** Available September 14, 2010.

#117 ONE NIGHT PREGNANCY
Lindsay Armstrong
Unexpected Babies

#118 SENSIBLE HOUSEKEEPER, SCANDALOUSLY PREGNANT
Jennie Lucas
Unexpected Babies

#119 FIRED WAITRESS, HIRED MISTRESS
Robyn Grady
Jet Set Billionaires

#120 PROPOSITIONED BY THE BILLIONAIRE
Lucy King
Jet Set Billionaires

HPECNM0810

GET 2 FREE LARGER-PRINT NOVELS PLUS 2 FREE GIFTS!

YES! Please send me 2 FREE LARGER-PRINT Harlequin Presents® novels and my 2 FREE gifts (gifts are worth about $10). After receiving them, if I don't wish to receive any more books, I can return the shipping statement marked "cancel". If I don't cancel, I will receive 6 brand-new novels every month and be billed just $4.55 per book in the U.S. or $5.24 per book in Canada. That's a saving of at least 13% off the cover price! It's quite a bargain! Shipping and handling is just 50¢ per book.* I understand that accepting the 2 free books and gifts places me under no obligation to buy anything. I can always return a shipment and cancel at any time. Even if I never buy another book, the two free books and gifts are mine to keep forever.

176/376 HDN E5NG

Name (PLEASE PRINT)

Address Apt. #

City State/Prov. Zip/Postal Code

Signature (if under 18, a parent or guardian must sign)

Mail to the **Harlequin Reader Service:**
IN U.S.A.: P.O. Box 1867, Buffalo, NY 14240-1867
IN CANADA: P.O. Box 609, Fort Erie, Ontario L2A 5X3

Not valid for current subscribers to Harlequin Presents Larger-Print books.

Are you a subscriber to Harlequin Presents books and want to receive the larger-print edition? Call 1-800-873-8635 today!

* Terms and prices subject to change without notice. Prices do not include applicable taxes. Sales tax applicable in N.Y. Canadian residents will be charged applicable provincial taxes and GST. Offer not valid in Quebec. This offer is limited to one order per household. All orders subject to approval. Credit or debit balances in a customer's account(s) may be offset by any other outstanding balance owed by or to the customer. Please allow 4 to 6 weeks for delivery. Offer available while quantities last.

Your Privacy: Harlequin Books is committed to protecting your privacy. Our Privacy Policy is available online at www.eHarlequin.com or upon request from the Reader Service. From time to time we make our lists of customers available to reputable third parties who may have a product or service of interest to you. If you would prefer we not share your name and address, please check here. ☐

Help us get it right—We strive for accurate, respectful and relevant communications. To clarify or modify your communication preferences, visit us at www.ReaderService.com/consumerschoice.

HPLP10R

Enjoy a sneak peek at fan favorite Molly O'Keefe's Harlequin Superromance miniseries, THE NOTORIOUS O'NEILLS, *with TYLER O'NEILL'S REDEMPTION, available September 2010 only from Harlequin Superromance.*

Police chief Juliette Tremblant recognized the shape of the man strolling down the street—in as calm and leisurely fashion as if it were the middle of the day rather than midnight. She slowed her car, convinced her eyes were playing tricks on her. It had been a long time since Tyler O'Neill had been seen in this town.

As she pulled to a stop at the curb, he turned toward her, and her heart about stopped.

"What the hell are you doing here, Tyler?"

"Well, if it isn't Juliette Tremblant." He made his way over to her, then leaned down so he could look her in the eye. He was close enough to touch.

Juliette was not, repeat, *not* going to touch Tyler O'Neill. Not with her fingers. Not with a ten-foot pole. There would be no touching. Which was too bad, since it was the only way she was ever going to convince herself the man standing in front of her—as rumpled and heart-stoppingly handsome now as he'd been at sixteen—was real.

And not a figment of all her furious revenge dreams.

"What are you doing back in Bonne Terre?" she asked.

"The manor is sitting empty," Tyler said and shrugged, as though his arriving out of the blue after ten years was casual. "Seems like someone should be watching over the family home."

"You?" She laughed at the very notion of him being here for any unselfish reason. "Please."

HSREXP0910

He stared at her for a second, then smiled. Her heart fluttered against her chest—a small mechanical bird powered by that smile.

"You're right." But that cryptic comment was all he offered.

Juliette bit her lip against the other questions.

Why did you go?

Why didn't you write? Call?

What did I do?

But what would be the point? Ten years of silence were all the answer she really needed.

She had sworn off feeling anything for this man long ago. Yet one look at him and all the old hurt and rage resurfaced as though they'd been waiting for the chance. That made her mad.

She put the car in gear, determined not to waste another minute thinking about Tyler O'Neill. "Have a good night, Tyler," she said, liking all the cool "go screw yourself" she managed to fit into those words.

It seems Juliette has an old score to settle with Tyler.
Pick up TYLER O'NEILL'S REDEMPTION
to see how he makes it up to her.
Available September 2010,
only from Harlequin Superromance.

Copyright © 2010 by Molly Fader

HSREXP0910

MARGARET WAY

introduces

The lives & loves of Australia's most powerful family

Growing up in the spotlight hasn't been easy, but the two Rylance heirs, Corin and his sister, Zara, have come of age and are ready to claim their inheritance. Though they are privileged, proud and powerful, they are about to discover that there are some things money can't buy....

Look for:

Australia's Most Eligible Bachelor

Available September

Cattle Baron Needs a Bride

Available October

www.eHarlequin.com

HR17679